A DEMON AND HIS PSYCHO

WELCOME TO HELL #2

EVE LANGLAIS

Copyright © July 2012, Eve Langlais

Cover Art by Dreams2Media July 2017

Produced in Canada

Published by Eve Langlais

www.EveLanglais.com

E-ISBN: 978-1-927459-08-9

Print ISBN: 978-1-988328-72-0

KDP ISBN: 978-1499198911

PROLOGUE

STRAPPED to the thick wooden chair – wearing a delightful, black and white striped, two piece outfit – her head shaved and gleaming, Katie giggled as she swung her feet. "Oops. You missed me. Missed me again," she sang. Minutes from her execution, her belly fully from her last meal – fried chicken, mashed potatoes, gravy and biscuits, mmmm – she was determined to make her last moments fun.

"Stay still," snapped the warden as he grabbed at her flailing limbs.

As if she'd start listening now, and to a pompous ass, no less. For three years now she'd clashed with her jailer. Arrogant prick, he always made a point to visit daily and count down the days to her demise. As soon as she could arrange it, she'd make him wish he'd treated her nicer. Then again, why wait?

Pointing her toes, clad only in thin socks, she bopped her jailor under the chin and heard his jaw snap with a clack. While she found his watering eyes entertaining, the warden didn't. He never did have much of a sense of humor, even when she painted clown faces – that looked remarkably like him down to the beady eyes and crooked nose – in her cell using the blood of the guard who thought she'd welcome his groping. Stupid warden; he didn't recognize her talent for laughter. Such a spoilsport.

Standing, red faced with his eyes narrowed in annoyance, the warden snapped his fingers and a pair of beefy males stepped forth.

"Ooh, a foursome. How kinky!" she exclaimed.

"Hold her!"

It took both guards to pin her legs to the chair – which was a step down from the six it took to get her into it in the first place. Give her a knife, even a small one, and they wouldn't have managed even that.

Wearing a satisfied smirk, the warden buckled the remaining leather straps around her. "Laugh your way out those. There's no escaping this time, Katie."

"That's what you think." How lovely. He blanched even though he believed he held the upper hand. A reputation for the impossible was a grand thing.

With no place to go – not with the way they tied her down; head, arms, legs and even her lap – she peeked around at the room. B-o-o-r-r-ring. All grey cement, exposed pipes and bare bulbs hanging on a wire. Really, given the audience the activities in this room drew, you'd think they'd dress it up a little.

Her chair – a wooden throne reserved for only the worst of the worst, a title she'd worked hard for – proved the most interesting thing. Plenty of famous people sat and died in the very same seat. None as cute as her, of course.

A thick cable – that would soon deliver her fate – snaked from a panel on the wall. The bulky cord split when it reached the chair into a number of smaller wires, which in turn, led to electrodes attached to her body. Currently turned off, the physical reminder of her impending death didn't hold her attention for long. Her gaze roved again and she smiled as she noted the sweating men who lined the room and avoided her gaze. Wimps.

"What? No goodbye kiss before you pull the switch?" she asked in a seemingly innocent voice. The warden and his staff knew better than to respond to her taunt. The new doctor they'd brought in didn't. His spectacled gaze met hers and she winked. "No touching my private girly parts after they fry me, doc, or else I might just come back to haunt you."

"I w-would never," he stuttered.

Her grin widened. "Why not? Aren't I pretty enough? All the boys I knew growing up thought so. And the guards. Of course, they can't admit that now." She lowered her voice. "I kind of killed them. But you seem nice. Want to give a condemned girl a last kiss?"

"I-um –"

Katie laughed as he turned red.

"Would you shut up?" hissed the warden. "This isn't a game. You're moments away from death. You should be thinking upon your crimes and what you did to deserve this punishment."

Her crimes? She chuckled even louder. "It isn't a crime to kill the wicked. And boy did I kill a lot of those."

Lips tight, the warden turned away and didn't answer her. No one ever did. No one ever wanted to admit she did the world at large a favor when she culled the evil

EVE LANGLAIS

ones who thought to hurt innocents. *I'm just a poor unrec-ognized hero, with a great smile – and killer moves.* She snickered.

Cranking a rope, the dusty curtain drew back from a large window, and surprise, an audience waited behind it. The seats were filled to capacity, both men and women alike, whispering and tittering as they waited in sick glee to see her jiggle like a bug on a hot plate.

She stuck her tongue out at them.

"Do you have any last words of remorse you'd like to share?" the warden asked through gritted teeth.

Last words? She leered at the priest who made the sign of the cross before looking away. The idiot in the collar wanted her to confess her sins and repent. The only thing she regretted was getting caught before killing some more.

"Thank you all for coming. I am sure some of you are silently cheering what you see as my impending demise. And I know some of you are imagining me naked. Perverts. To you all I say –" She paused for effect, glancing around the room and meeting the eyes of those who dared. "I can't wait to see you in Hell! Kiss my ass motherfu –"

Thousands of volts of electricity slammed into her and her teeth clacked together as her body trembled. But even in pain and about to meet her maker, she couldn't help but choke out a wheezing laugh. She howled as she died. Cackled as her spirit sank into the otherworld. She giggled as she took the boat, manned by the super famous Charon, across the Styx to her new world, and life. Arriving at the bank of the innermost circle of Hell, her mirth finally tapered off.

4

A sprawling metropolis stretched in front of her, the stone and brick of the walls stained from the ash raining feather light, all around. A sniff of the air and she wrinkled her nose as the stench of brimstone pervaded. Already, her two-piece prison-wear clung to her as the heat of the Pit embraced her.

"Ahem."

Disturbed from her first glimpse of Hell, Katie turned to see who wanted her attention.

A distinguished gent with silver temples and fire in his eyes waited for her on the mooring dock. He held out his hand and she took the firm grip as she stepped from the boat.

"Welcome to Hell, dearest Katie. You've been eagerly anticipated."

Peering up at Satan, his smile filled with genuine warmth, his presence a soothing balm after a life spent either hiding or hunting, she relaxed.

"It's great to finally be here." And it was, because as the newest member of Lucifer's legion – she ensured her spot when she signed that contract in blood years ago – she could do what she did best. Kill the unworthy.

Smiling wide, the chuckles returned, but this time, she didn't laugh alone.

THE GIGGLE FLOATED to him from above, light, and cheerful. A promise of mischief.

Xaphan ignored it. In Lucifer's castle, strange noises occurred all the time. He'd grown used to the madness on the rare times he visited, and preferred to avoid it. Getting involved just wasn't his thing. Besides, he had an appointment with his Lord, and Xaphan loathed tardiness.

The high pitched laughter grew closer, echoing down the swirling staircase, along with an exuberant, "Whee!" An odd swishing noise joined the exuberant giggling and Xaphan finally flicked his gaze upward in time to see the most bizarre sight ever.

A female, dressed in a pair of indecently cut jean shorts with a pink blouse tied off under her bosom, displaying a rounded naval where a piercing glinted, came surfing down the banister. Coasting the narrow stone, her arms windmilled as she hopped over the newel post that marked the second floor landing. One foot came up and she balanced precariously, her speed increasing as she continued her descent.

"Uh-oh," she exclaimed as she wobbled. Her eyes widened, her long, blonde pig tails fluttered, and Xaphan sighed.

Lunatic. He turned away, not interested in seeing the crash, but he whirled back at her yelled, "Catch me!" Forgoing the remaining feet of railing, the blonde psycho launched herself straight at him.

"What the fuck!" One hundred and sixty pounds – a weight he knew well from his endurance and muscle building sessions – of giggling female hit him. Her legs wrapped around his waist while her hands clutched his shoulders. A shrill squeal of delight deafened him. He staggered under the unexpected burden and his hands automatically grasped at her. The touch of her smooth flesh – a perfect handful – made his skin sizzle on contact.

"Yippee, that was fun!" the lunatic exclaimed, bouncing in his grip.

"For who?" he muttered, juggling, whether he liked it or not, the wiggly body in his arms. A very nice body, with plush breasts that rubbed against his chest, and full ass cheeks made to cushion a man's thrusting body.

"Nice catch by the way," she added with a naughty grind of her lower parts against his. Damn his cock for waking up with more interest than her antic should have merited.

"Did I have a choice?"

"A true gentleman never lets a lady fall."

Him? A gentleman? Now that was funny. But not as funny as her other comment. "Where's the lady?"

A brilliant green eye, and a clear blue one, regarded him and the tip of her pink tongue peeked out to lick full lips. "Good point," she giggled, not offended at all. "But a girl likes to pretend."

To that, he didn't have a retort, but he did have to fight a smile. *She's crazy, but cute.* And sexy, he revised as she again wiggled against him, a deadly combination for males who were available to the fairer sex. Thankfully, he was not, so he fought off her allure. Or tried to, at least. Certain parts of his body didn't seem keen on cooperating.

It didn't help when she gave him a look over, which involved scanning his features, leaning over to check out his ass, then bouncing her butt again which put pressure on a part currently borrowing more of this blood than he liked. He blamed the lack of hemoglobin to his brain for his inability to drop the psycho on her butt.

A twinkle – a naughty one promising delights he'd foresworn – shone in her eyes. "Nice to meet you, handsome. Lady or not, aren't you glad you were in the right place at the right time?"

"Not really." Words that screamed *lie,* seeing as how he had yet to let her go. Madness. Pure madness, and he blamed it on her scent, a vanilla like flavor which surrounded him and made his mouth water for a taste.

She smiled at his dry retort and her eyes crinkled with mischief. "And yet your grip is so *firm.*" She chuckled, a husky sound that touched him like a caress. "I have to say, though, landing on you is almost like hitting the floor. All *hard* and *unyielding.*" She emphasized her words with a wiggle, which, even he could grudgingly admit, would have worked better naked.

With a growl, more with annoyance at himself than her sly innuendo, he set her down – against his cock's wishes. "Be more careful. The next time there might not be someone there to catch you."

"Yes, daddy." A smirk twisted her lips. "Wanna punish me?" Whirling around, she presented him her back and bent over, her rounded ass sticking up, the short bottoms she wore exposing way too much creamy skin.

The things I could do to her in that position. Hips thrusting...Bodies slapping... He shook the thought away, and clenched his fists at his side lest he give in to temptation and give her what she asked for; a good smack on those cheeks. But in her case it wouldn't be punishment he guessed. Cock teases like her were always trying to tempt a demon. However, he knew how to abstain, even if he could so easily imagine tearing the tiny bit of fabric off her sex and pumping into her for a good, hard fuck.

She shook her butt at him. "I'm waiting," she sang.

You'll be waiting a long time then. Not interested in playing her game, despite his erection, he walked away, the thump of his boots on the floor a loud echo in the hall.

"Hey, tall, dark and gloomy, where are you going?" she asked catching up to him and then skipping alongside in her pristine Reebok sneakers.

"I have an appointment with our Lord."

"Oooh. Going to see the big boss man. Are you in trouble?"

"No."

"Asking for a raise?"

"No."

"Going for a man-on-man quickie?"

The crude inquiry made him stumble. "Most definitely not."

"So you like girls?" She bounced in front of him and cocked her head as she asked. He swept around her.

"Hey! You didn't answer me."

"Because I am ignoring you," he snapped. "Don't you have some other demon to bother?"

"Nope."

"A place to be?"

"Have you changed your mind about putting me on top of your cock? You're big enough, I bet I could spin."

"No!" Oh fuck him, but he could picture it though. Bad. Bad. Bad. Was the female part succubus to tempt him so? In his three hundred years in Hell, he'd never had to fight an attraction to the women who constantly tried to seduce him. Never had someone who made him think such lustful thoughts. It shamed him which in turn angered him. "Would you go away and leave me alone?"

To his dismay, she kept pace with him, humming off key as she skipped. He knew he should keep his lips sealed. Knew he should just mind his business, but... "Why are you following me?"

"I also have an appointment with the boss."

Xaphan shot a look at her and wondered what Lucifer could want with the flighty creature who tortured him by refusing to go away. "Are you his new girlfriend?"

"Me? Good grief no. Mother Earth would skin me alive and use me as fertilizer if I dared make a move on her man. I work for him."

"Doing what?" What could a blonde airhead like her do other than strip and dance on a pole while demons threw money at her?

"I do this and that. Boring stuff for a big, bad demon like yourself." She batted her lashes at him. He snorted at her not so subtle attempt to soften him up. "You know, I don't think I gave you my name," she said.

"Because I didn't ask." And didn't care. He'd gone several hundred years without meeting her. He now hoped to go several hundred more before he did again, despite the fact she was the first female he'd felt such an instant attraction for since the loss of his one, true love. Thankfully, his work tended to take him mortal–side, so his chances of running into the psycho again after today were slim to none.

"Such a polite demon. But I can tell you're dying to know. I'm Katie."

"Now that I know, I'm sure I'll sleep better tonight."

"Sleep? Not if I'm in bed with you." She skipped ahead and winked over her shoulder.

Instant images, carnal ones of course, crawled through his brain – of Katie naked, over him, her breasts jiggling as she rode. Under him, lips parted in invitation. Bent over...

He clamped his eyes shut and counted, tuning her out. Or trying to. Something she babbled caught his attention despite his attempt. "Excuse me?"

"I said, aren't you coming?"

No, but he wanted to. However, she wasn't talking about the cock spewing version of come, but the arrived-at-their-destination one. Seeing the large carved door to his Lord's outer office and reception, Xaphan almost sighed with relief and restrained an urge to dive for cover from the crazy blonde.

"We're here," she announced, clapping her hands.

"Thank Hell," he muttered. "If you don't mind, I'm almost late for my meeting. Goodbye, Katie." Striding into the outer vestibule, he gave a curt nod to the Lord's wrinkled hag of a secretary. She waved him in and he didn't hesitate, eager to escape Katie and her innumerable questions – and his strange reaction to her presence.

His Lord's office was a quiet haven. With a high ceiling arching overhead, a gleaming stone floor, and walls adorned in tapestries depicting epic battles, it was a true man's cave, right down to the desk carved out of some massive jawbone of a creature long extinct. Behind the ivory monstrosity, piled high with papers, sat his boss.

Clacking his heels to attention, Xaphan's leather armor – a.k.a. his reinforced motorcycle jacket, which he removed only to bathe and sleep, and was a heck of a lot more comfortable than the chain mail of old – creaked as he waited for Lucifer to notice him. The Lord of the Pit, dressed in his golfing attire of red and black plaid shorts and a collared shirt patterned to resemble flames, finished writing with a flourish and set aside his quill. Leaning back in his massive chair, his boss folded his hands over his chest and regarded him with hooded eyes.

"Xaphan, how nice of you to drop by."

"You ordered me to, sir."

"So I did. And of course you obeyed being such a well behaved demon. I like that in a soldier. Such a refreshing change from some of my other minions, and children. Ungrateful brats. Sit down, boy."

Xaphan seated himself in the massive wingback chair facing the desk.

"So tell me, how have you been?"

Great. Lucifer was in one of his chit-chat moods. "Fine."

"Just fine? Come on, surely a good looking demon, like yourself, has some exciting stuff going on? Maybe a new girlfriend?"

Xaphan frowned. "My Lord knows I made a vow to never love another. I keep my word."

"I know." Those two words dripped with disgust. "It's the thing I dislike most about you. But thankfully you make up for that character lapse in other ways."

"Thank you. I think." As usual, following Lucifer's twisted thought process proved interesting. Yet, despite his Lord's odd logic, Xaphan had learned over the centuries to like and respect him. Sure, he incarnated everything evil in the world, but, when you got past the whole Satan façade, he truly was an interesting person and a fair boss, so long as a minion did his job.

"So listen, I called you here for a reason. I've got a mission to give you, a very important one, and I'll tell you all about it when your partner arrives."

"I work alone."

"Usually, but not this time. Don't worry though. I'm sure she'll be an asset where you're going."

"She?" A sinking feeling clutched him. No. It couldn't be.

"Hi, boss. I'm here! Aren't you just so excited to see me? I know I would be. And look who else showed up. My new friend, stick in the mud. Hi!" Katie threw Xaphan a cheery wave and a toothy smile.

Xaphan ignored her. Or at least tried to. He averted his eyes, but his dick immediately swelled to attention. It seemed to like her around. He'd beat it later – in punishment, not pleasure.

A smile hovering around his lips, Lucifer waved her closer. "I see you've met your partner."

Lips pulled down in a grimace, Xaphan answered. "Unfortunately. You expect me to work with her? You can't be serious?"

"Oh but I am," Lucifer replied with a smile that sent the damned – the smart ones at any rate – running.

Smart or not, Xaphan wasn't giving in without a fight. "Like fuck. I am not working with that crazy female."

"Why not?" she asked with a pout, planting her hands on her hips.

It was ridiculously cute, and proved his point. "Exactly how are you supposed to help? Look at you."

She peered down and rotated her hips, trying to look behind her. "What about me? Is it the shorts? Did I not trim enough off? I skipped the underwear so I wouldn't have any lines. It's the bra, isn't it? I went for support so I wouldn't jiggle when I ran, but you're right. It's got to go." And it did. A shimmy, a wink and a wiggle later, a black lace confection went whipping towards his face.

He caught it, stunned. "You're completely and utterly psycho."

"Why thank you," she said, as she held a hand to her chest and preened. "I do try my best."

"That she does," Lucifer agreed. "Which is why I think she'll be a perfect match for the task I've got planned."

"I am so winning employee of the year this time," Katie exclaimed, punctuated with a fist pump.

With matching lunatic smiles, his boss and the psycho faced him. Xaphan shook his head. "You can't be serious.

How am I supposed to work with that?" Oblivious again, Katie twirled her hair as she danced in place to music only she could hear.

"Despite her exterior, I assure you she is quite lethal."

Shooting Lucifer a look of incredulity, Xaphan replied, "How? Does her nonstop giggles and irritating chatter make her prey kill themselves?"

"No, my knives keep accidentally ending up in demon bodies. I have anger issues," Katie said, dropping her head and scuffing her toes. "But I'm working on them. I've only killed one demon this week."

"I'm afraid to ask why," he muttered.

"He totally deserved it," she retorted.

"Of course he did," Lucifer interjected in a soothing tone. "And while I do so enjoy watching your skill with a blade, this time, instead of killing things, I need you to find something."

"Treasure?" she asked, perking up with interest.

"No."

"Long lost son?"

"No. I know where that annoying brat is"

"Wedding ring?"

"I've not gotten that far yet," Lucifer muttered. "Gaia says we need to work on communication. Meanwhile she's the one who disappears every time we get in a yelling match."

"And yet a good holler now and then is good for the relationship," Katie replied sagely.

"I know. But does Mother Earth see it that way? Oh no, it's always tell me how you're feeling, and what do I think about blah blah blah," he mimed in a high voice.

"Poor boss," she sympathized. "At least my demon

partner here and I won't have that problem. He's already got the hollering part down pat. I can't wait to see how he is with the makeup sex."

"We are not having sex," Xaphan growled. "And we're not partners."

"Oh yes you are, unless you'd prefer latrine duty?" Lucifer said with a benign smile at odds with the flames glowing in his eyes.

"What's the mission?" The idea of pairing with Katie annoyed him, but anything beat the latrines. Damned demons didn't have any fucking aim.

"My granddaughter lost her dragon."

Lucifer wanted him to look for a pet? How degrading. "So buy her a new one."

"Now that's just mean," Katie huffed. "As if the little girl wouldn't know the difference."

"Exactly." Lucifer nodded. "Not to mention, while I usually condone stealing, that applies to everyone else. Stealing from me on the other hand is completely unacceptable. Someone needs to pay." He pulled out a folder, a slim one, with several sheets of paper and on top, a photo. Katie got her hands on it before Xaphan could get a peek. "Here's what I know. The dragon was last seen in the stone garden chewing on some lava rocks. Then nothing."

"Did it fly away?"

The pair of eyes that turned Xaphan's way, filled with incredulity, made him frown. "What? Dragons have wings. It's not an unreasonable question."

Mismatched eyes rolled and Katie shook her head at him. "It's a baby. Like duh. Only adult dragons can fly."

"Well how was I supposed to know it wasn't full grown?"

EVE LANGLAIS

"Because a full grown dragon wouldn't chew on rocks, silly. Only teething babies do."

"See, she's proving to be an asset already," Lucifer exclaimed, rubbing his hands together. "I knew I was making the right choice pairing you up."

"You're both insane," he muttered.

"Thank you," they replied in chorus.

And despite himself, Xaphan's lips almost twitched a smile in response. He clamped his mouth tight. *I don't smile. Even for cute psychopaths.*

KATIE WAS ENJOYING HERSELF WAY TOO MUCH. SOMETHING about the staid demon brought out the imp in her, and the more he scowled, the more she goaded him. It didn't hurt that the partner Lucifer assigned her now owned a heading in her mental dictionary under *super yummy*.

Taller than her by a good foot or more, the serious male sported dark locks that hung around his face, an unshaven jaw and a body so toned and hard, even she was impressed. Dressed in a leather jacket, which seemed to double as armor, skin tight pants and shit-kicking boots, his bad boy look totally rocked.

Even better, despite how much she annoyed him, he'd not laid one finger on her – although if he did, she'd break it. An unabashed cock tease, Katie loved to drive males insane, then killed them if they crossed the line. Although of late, she was trying to cut down on the number of permanent deaths she meted, and tried to stick to severe maiming instead – Lucifer complained she was hurting his efforts to rebuild his army. But that wasn't the only reason. Her psychiatrist said she needed to learn to temper her responses to situations where demons took liberties with her person. Apparently, murderous rampages weren't healthy. But they sure were fun.

Lucky for her, while she had to tone down the violence in her private life, Lucifer gave her plenty of opportunities to vent. She was his very own enforcer sent on the worst missions to take care of escapees, usually into the wilds of Hell, where her deadly nature thrived.

Except for this time. The boss had a different purpose for her. No killing or maiming on the menu. Instead, he expected her to find a dragon. And odder, he wanted her to partner with a demon, a demon who wanted nothing to do with her. She did so love a challenge.

"I work better alone," the grumpy male said, still not willing to accept it was fate they work together.

"Are you defying me?" Lucifer said it quietly, but she and the demon both felt the underlying power lacing his words.

Her new partner grumbled. He scowled. He made his displeasure known aloud. However, in the end, her grumpy demon obeyed Lucifer, and Katie exited the office at her new partner's heels ready to see how far she could push him before he snapped.

"So where are we going first? Armory to get some sharp and pointy weapons?"

"No."

"Kitchen to fill our little tummies?"

"No."

"Mmm, how about that alcove around the corner for some hanky-panky?"

The last suggestion saw his nostrils flare, his bearing

turn even more rigid and his lips stretched so tight, she wondered if they would split. "We have a job to do so get your mind out of the gutter and focus."

"But the gutter is so much fun," she pointed out. "Spoilsport. Fine. Since you don't like any of my ideas, what do you think we should do?"

"I thought *I* would speak to the dragon's caretaker."

"Yay. We're going to the kennels. Do you know Throat Ripper just had a litter of hellhounds? Cute little buggers. If I wasn't so attached to my toes, I'd get one."

A heavy sigh was his reply.

Skipping beside him, she grinned at the glower gracing his countenance. Oh, she could already predict the fun she would have bugging him. Humming off key, just because she liked the way he gritted his teeth, she let him lead the way to the kennels. She let herself lag behind to check out the view from behind. It was prime beef, even with his rigid gait.

Before she could come up with a way to get him to bend over, exposing his ass for a slap that would surely make him bellow, they arrived at their destination.

"Katie!" Ricco, the head honcho of the Lord's kennels, saw them arrive and waved from the pen where he worked. A giant of a male, half demon, half troll, what Ricco lacked in looks – and hygiene – he made up for in friendly personality.

"Hey Ricco. How's it going?"

"You know how it is. Thirteen stitches yesterday. Twenty five the day before. Throat Ripper's litter is giving me the usual training problems." No sooner did he mention it, than snarls erupted. Diving down, Ricco reappeared a moment later holding a pair of slavering, coal colored pups by the scruff. "No eating each other," he admonished. "Save it for later when we go to the penal yard. I hear we've got a big batch of bad souls in need of manners."

"Darn it. I wish I could stay for the show." What a shame she had work to do. She did so enjoy watching the damned souls – those here on minor sins – who thought they could disobey their Lord's laws. Living in Hell didn't mean a soul could do whatever they pleased. Lucifer had rules, lots of them, and if an idiot broke one, like defacing one of his many statue tributes, he punished the culprits. Herding the miscreants into the kennel's penal yard for the puppies to practice their skills on was just one of his devious solutions to get the billions of souls inhabiting Hell to behave.

But that punishment was for the minors. The truly wicked got to live in the prison where torture was a form of art. Sometimes, when feeling particularly inspired, she visited and dispensed her artistic vision on the evil souls residing there. The screams she recorded on her I-pod made for great background music when she went for her daily walk.

"I'll video tape it for you, lassie" the kennel keeper promised. "But, judging by your serious faced friend, I'd wager you're here for something other than enter-tainment."

"Our Lord has assigned us the task of locating the missing dragon belonging to his granddaughter." Xaphan announced their mission in a monotone voice.

"And you're our first suspect!" she chirped. "So fess up."

Ricco knew her well enough to chuckle. "Not much to

tell, lassie. The princess's dragon is a well behaved beast and a joy to take care of. On the day she disappeared, I took her as usual to the garden for her daily rock chewing."

"Why not just feed her the rocks here?" Xaphan interrupted.

A shrug lifted the beefy keeper's shoulders. "It doesn't work as well, not unless you've got a wide variety. A growing dragon needs all kinds of lava rocks to cut their teeth and supplement their diet, and while the wee critter has a stall for sleeping and a pen leading off that so she can get outside for some air, none are big enough to really handle the amount of stones required. The Lord's garden, already being well established with a large number of them, plus the room needed for the wee thing to stretch its legs, seemed like a perfect solution. It was that or we'd have to send the critter to the mountains, which Lucifer's granddaughter wouldn't have liked at all. Not to mention, her mama doesn't like her young'un going anywhere outside the castle."

"Okay so now that we've established the necessity, did you see anything out of the ordinary that day? Men in dark suits? Midgets in cowls? Anything?" She ignored the incredulous look Xaphan shot her.

"Nope. I took the wee dragon into the garden, locked the door behind me, and came back to fetch her at the end of the day only to discover she was gone."

Frowning, Xaphan asked the next question. "Was the door still locked?"

"Aye. And no one borrowed my key, which I keep hung around my neck." Ricco pulled on a chain and showed them the massive, ornate key.

"Who else would have access to the garden?"

Again, Ricco shrugged. "Everyone. We only locked it when the wee thing was in there for its feeding."

"So who else has a key?"

Xaphan's query sounded accusatory, and Ricco bristled. "How would I know? I'm just the hired help."

"What do you think happened, Ricco? I'm going with aliens. Maybe they beamed the dragon out and are going to probe it."

"Or maybe someone took it and intends to use it for ransom. Oh wait, that smacks of logic. That can't be right," Xaphan said in a mocking tone.

"If I'm right, I am going to make you eat crow, and unlike that king in that poem, they won't be baked in a pie."

"The nursery rhyme refers to black birds."

"Same thing."

"Is not."

"Is too," she stated planting her hands on her hips.

"Actually, lad, she's right."

"That's got to be a first," he muttered.

Being a gracious winner, she stuck her tongue out at him.

His eyes glinted, but he didn't reply, and instead, turned to Ricco. "Thank you, sir, for answering our questions."

"I hope ye find the wee dragon. I was kind of fond of her. She's the only pet I've kept in the past century who hasn't tried to eat any of my body parts."

Waving goodbye, Katie skipped after Xaphan as he strode out of the kennel area. "So partner, where to next?"

"Lunch. My body requires sustenance."

23

"Why not just say you're hungry?"

"Fine. I'm hungry. Happy? Now if you don't mind, I'm going to eat before continuing."

"Sounds like a great idea. I think better on a full stomach."

"When you think at all."

He barely whispered the words, but she heard them and took offense. Sticking her foot out, she snickered when he stumbled.

"Would you stop fucking around?" he snarled.

"Why? I'm having fun."

"But, I'm not."

"That's because you need to lighten up."

"I'd prefer you left me alone."

"No can do, grumpy. Lucifer said we are partners on this job, so whether you like it or not, I am going to stay glued by your side. So suck it up buttercup and learn to love me."

"That would take a miracle," he grumbled.

"Or a few blows to the head," she quipped. "So where are we going to lunch? Are you in the mood for a sixty nine? I could go for some sausage." Ooh what fun. The vein in his forehead throbbed.

"I am going to the kitchen for food. Real food." He enunciated very clearly despite his gritted teeth.

"Oh, that is so romantic. You, cooking for me on our first work date." She batted her lashes when she smiled at him.

"This is not a date!" He practically shouted it.

She patted his cheek. "If you say so, grumpy."

A growl rumbled from deep within him.

Biting her lower lip held the laughter in, barely. She

knew she shouldn't bait the poor fellow, but really, he made it too easy.

Lunch passed with her annoying him as much as possible, and him glowering at his sandwich. But she had to admire his control. Even when she threw popcorn at his head, stole his drink and chugged it, and kicked the stool out from under him, he didn't snap. Glared at her. Muttered under his breath. Growled. But he didn't once lift a hand to rebuke her. How fascinating.

Done with their meal, he even cleaned up! Katie rubbed her eyes because she thought she hallucinated. "Are you for real?" she asked in disbelief.

"If I say no, will you pretend I don't exist and go away?"

She shook her head and he sighed. "You know, you might act all uptight and grim, but I think deep down inside..." He arched a brow and she added, "Really deep down, I think you might have a sense of humor."

"And deep down inside, I think you're still a psycho."

She beamed. "Consistency is my middle name. So, where to next, partner?"

"I am going to look at the scene of the crime. Join me or not, I don't care."

"Crime? We don't know yet if it was a crime or an escape. We need clues before jumping to assumptions."

"Why don't I look for clues while you do something else?" he suggested.

"Like what?"

"I don't know. Maybe make some posters. Didn't Lucifer give you a picture? I'm sure we can find some crayons and paper for you somewhere."

Oh ho, her demon threw another barb with his dry

sense of humor. She liked it. "Art makes me angry."

"Then use a photocopier."

Holding up the picture from the file, she eyed the cute bugger posed beside Lucifer's granddaughter. "It's a waste of time. Somehow, I think if someone found it wandering around, they would have returned it."

"Why?"

She held out the image and he glanced at it. Did a double take and shook his head. "Pink? We're looking for a fucking pink dragon? That can't be natural."

"It's not," she advised. "Dragons are green, grey, white, black or blue. Usually. But, rumor is that Lucifer had his girlfriend Gaia change the DNA strand for its color, hence the rather pretty shade of pink. I think it's sweet."

"I think it's cruel," he muttered. "A pink carnivore! What is Hell coming to?"

Smirking at his back – while admiring the muscles flexing in his ass as he walked – she followed, and wondered herself at their odd pairing. It wasn't that Lucifer didn't give her strange jobs. He did, quite often actually, but they usually involved killing things. And she did those deeds by herself.

This time though, no killing, maiming or removing of body parts was expected. And her boss paired her with Mr. Uptight, who had yet to give her his name.

"So what's your name?"

"Does it really matter?"

"Of course it does. I need something to yell when you try to touch me later."

Ah, she'd finally pushed the right button. He whirled on her and, in a blink, had her pressed against the wall, hands bracketing her body while he glared down at her.

"I. Am. Not. Going. To. Fuck. You." He enunciated each word very clearly.

He possessed great diction. She giggled. Dick. What a funny word. "I'm sorry, would you prefer the term made love to?"

"No." He just about shouted it. "I have no interest in you as a woman. At all. Ever. None. So stop with the sexual jokes."

"You don't?" She eyed him with curiosity from his blazing eyes, to the hard set of his jaw, the rigid stance of his shoulders, and finally, to the hard bulge at his groin. "Funny, because either you're horny or that's some wicked cod piece you've got hiding in your pants."

No. It couldn't be. Not here. Not in Hell. It was. A blush on the demon's cheeks. She'd never thought to see the day. She almost peeked outside to see if Hell froze over – again. Someone really needed to come up with a better expression because it just didn't have the same effect anymore. Maybe they could change it to when her grumpy partner finally laughed.

"It's adrenaline," he lied. Idiot, like she didn't know the difference between a hard on she caused versus a battle fever one. "Now, if you'll excuse me, I've got a mission to complete." Left unsaid was '…and a partner to ditch.' As if she'd let him escape so easily.

Despite her initial surprise at Lucifer's command, she couldn't help but find herself intrigued by the staid soldier. *I wonder what it would take to make him smile? Or make him change his mind about fucking?* Because he'd done the one thing he shouldn't have. The one thing guaranteed to peak her interest. He'd said no.

And she wanted to find out why.

2

ENTERING THE PALACE ROCK GARDEN, Xaphan tried to ignore Katie at his back, but she didn't make it easy. Her scent – oh sweet fucking vanilla, a delicious treat that just lacked him on top – kept swirling around him, rousing a carnal hunger he'd not experienced in so long. She bounced ahead and made a pretense of bending over to look under and around the rocks adorning the courtyard. Each peek of her ass, spilling from her shorts in tempting white globes, made his cock twitch.

But he would control himself. Reign in his lusty urge and not give in to temptation, after all, she wasn't even his type. Yeah, he could tell himself that all he wanted, it did nothing to remove the blood from his groin. He tried to picture his lost love's face in the hopes of calming his erection, but he couldn't bring her to mind. Not even her soft gaze. Instead, a smirk with mismatched eyes kept superimposing itself. It made him terse.

"The dragon's not hiding under a fucking rock," he snapped.

Bent over again, she peered at him over her shoulder. "Well duh. I'm looking for an escape route."

"Come again?"

Straightening, she smiled. "I thought you'd never ask."

"Stick to the job," he growled.

"Oh alright, spoilsport. Let's look at what we know. The dragon was in the garden for its daily outdoor exercise. When the dragon keeper returned, it was gone."

"This doesn't explain why you're looking under rocks."

She rolled her eyes. "Because you didn't let me finish. Isn't that just like a man? But, I was saying, no one saw the dragon leaving this room."

"So the perp had it in a bag. Or a box."

"You'd have to be pretty big and strong to carry the dragon. Even babies weigh a ton. Not to mention, the camera footage shows no one entering or leaving the garden via any of the exits."

"How do you know this?" And yeah, he sounded suspicious.

Holding up the sheet Lucifer gave them, she smirked. "Because I actually read the report."

"When did you have a chance? You haven't left my bloody side since we exited Lucifer's office."

"I read it while we were walking, of course, silly. Or did you think I spent that entire time checking out your ass?"

Did she like what she saw? No, strike that. He didn't care. "How could you be reading when you yacked the entire time?"

"Some of us know how to multi task. It comes in handy in bed."

Xaphan closed his eyes and heard her giggle. It was

fast proving the most annoying – and arousing – sound ever. "Can we get back to our task?"

"You started it when you asked how I could have possibly read the report. Not my fault I'm more prepared for this job than you are."

"I would have read it too if someone wasn't hogging it," he replied, annoyed at himself that he'd not thought to look it over first, before she got her small hands on it.

"Ask me nicely, and I'll let you have a peek."

"Stop playing your games and hand it over."

"Say please."

"Please," he growled.

"Pretty please with a cherry on top."

"Give it to me right fucking now," he bellowed.

Shaking her head, she tsked him. "Bad demon. That was rude. If you want it, come and get it." The minx then stuffed it down her shirt.

Before he could have time to tell himself what a bad idea it was, he stalked over to her. As he reached out to grab her, she darted away with a giggle.

"Get back here," he snarled.

"Run, run as fast as you can, you can't catch me, I'm a hell-ion." She sang the rhyme then skipped away.

But Xaphan didn't play games, or chase blonde hotties who teased him. Screw the report. He'd just rely on old fashioned investigating. Ignoring her, he instead crouched and surveyed the ground of the garden. Most of the surface held a layer of soot and ash, a quirk of Hell created by the furnace which kept this plane smoking hot.

Observing the scuff of feet along the twining paths, he scouted, looking for… Aha! The patch of dirt stood out from all the others because of its pristine evenness.

Someone had taken a broom to wipe the tracks, but in doing so left their first clue. The swipe marks stopped at a huge boulder. It seemed immovable, but he could see the crumbles of dirt that tunneled up into ridges around the bottom.

Putting his shoulder to the slab, he pushed. It didn't budge. Inhaling deep, he dug in his heels and heaved again.

"What are you doing?" Katie watched him, twirling her hair again.

"What does it look like I'm doing?" he replied through gritted teeth.

"Like you're trying to muscle that huge rock aside."

"Someone moved it once already so it's possible." If he just dug a little deeper and applied a little more strength…

"I don't think that's working."

No, it wasn't, which irritated him. He prided himself on his strength. Worked out every day as a matter of fact. Yet, he couldn't budge one fucking boulder. "Got a better idea?"

"Actually I do." Stepping close to him, close enough he could see down her shirt and note the piece of paper caught between her breasts, she reached up over his shoulder and pressed her bosom against his chest, making him inadvertently rumble – whether in discontent or pleasure, he couldn't tell.

The rumble grew louder and shook him. What the fuck? He jumped aside as the stone at his back shifted revealing a dark maw.

"How did you know where that lever was?" he asked suspiciously.

"A friend told me about it a while back," she said with a smug smile.

"You could have mentioned it before." Before he'd grunted and heaved like an idiot.

"And miss the floor show?" Pearly white teeth shone as she smiled. "Next time though, do it shirtless would you?"

With an impish wink, she ducked into the tunnel. Xaphan followed, a string of curses on his tongue, but he didn't say them. To respond to her teasing would just invite more. If he ignored her, she would tire of the game and move onto harassing someone else.

Why that idea pissed him off, he couldn't have said.

LEADING THE WAY, KATIE WALKED THE TUNNEL, LIGHTING A dusty torch she found in a bracket to illuminate their path. While the walls and ceiling of the hidden passage were covered in the tracks of time, in other words, dust and sticky cobwebs, the floor itself showed signs of recent use. The trail with its scuffed evidence of many feet and a slithery tail sliding along behind showed them on the right track. Problem was, if her source was right, she knew where the path led. And they weren't ready for it.

"We should turn back," she said after several minutes of treading – well, skipping on her part – in the darkness barely held at bay by the sputtering torch.

"Why? Is someone scared of the dark?" he mocked.

"No."

"Break a nail?"

"No." But she had to smile as he tried to goad her.

"Cold because you forgot to wear actual clothes?"

"Actually a little," she admitted, Hell's usual heat not easily penetrating this enclosed space. "Thanks for offering to help."

"What?"

With no warning, she thrust the torch into a crevice in the wall, then launched herself at him, wrapping herself around his body.

"What are you doing?" he asked in an oddly tight voice.

"Using you for heat. Although, this would work better if you wore less layers. I hear naked, skin to skin works best."

"Get off me."

"Isn't the proper term, get me off?"

Muttering curses under his breath, he tried to peel her off. But like an octopus, she kept slapping a limb around him, clinging tight. After several minutes of tussling, and bouncing, which had her more excited than she would have expected, he stopped.

"Will you get off if I promise to give you my coat?"

"You'd let me wear it?" Given how the item fit him like a second skin, she doubted he meant it.

"If you're truly that cold, then yes." Just saying he would seemed to pain him, and curious, she let herself slide from his body. Standing before him expectantly, she waited for him to laugh and tell her he lied. It's what men did after all. Promise a girl fidelity, then cheat with her best friend. Tell a girl he'd respect her in the morning and not return her calls. Men were such predictable pigs.

To her eye widening surprise, Xaphan unzipped his jacket and slid it off. He then draped the heavy coat over her shoulders, the warmth of his body seeping into her skin. His crisp clean scent comprised of a strong soap and *man*, enveloped her. A chill that had nothing to do with her body, thawed. She peered up at him in wonderment.

"You gave me your coat."

"Loaned," he corrected. "I expect it returned once we leave, and next time, try to dress for the occasion."

Speaking of dressed, she noted with interest the Henley shirt he wore, black of course, clinging to his well-defined upper body. *I'll have to think of way to get him to peel that one off too, next time.* Because despite knowing firsthand how despicable men could be, how they hurt, and lied, and didn't care, Xaphan intrigued her. He was unlike other males she'd encountered. A puzzle she wanted to unravel.

And fuck. That last realization surprised her most of all.

3

BACK AT HIS PLACE, an hour later, Xaphan paced as he tried to figure out what happened. One minute he traded barbs with the psycho known as Katie, the next he wore her, like a living blanket. And by all the lives he'd taken, he'd wanted to wrap his arms around her and still the faint shivering in her chilled frame. He'd wanted to warm her plush body with hot kisses and caresses until they both fairly burned. To seek the hot core hidden between her legs, pumping them both to sweaty ecstasy. Instead, he managed to convince her to take his coat, which surprised the hell out of her.

He'd not missed the shock on her face when he'd draped it around her body, its large size swimming on her in a way that made her look fragile – and ridiculously cute. He noted how she kept turning her face into the collar and rubbing her cheek against it as they trekked back to the garden. He'd welcomed her explanation, not couched in her usual innuendo, that they needed supplies before continuing their journey. Apparently she knew of

EVE LANGLAIS

the path they found, and with a serious mien – a welcome
change from her usually exuberant and inappropriate
conversation – listed the items they'd need to bring. Then
she took off, still wearing his coat, promising to meet him
in a few hours.

He'd welcomed the excuse to lose her for a while.
Despite his usual iron control, he wasn't sure how much
longer he could trust himself to keep his hands off of her.
Less than a day since they'd met and a vow he'd made
over three hundred years ago held by only a thread.

The shame of it made him drop to his knees before the
small portrait he'd stolen so long ago. "Forgive me,
Roxanne. I am not worthy of your love." He never was,
not that she ever cared.

As a poor knight, and a bastard to boot, he'd only
wished to serve his king and lord. Then he met Roxanne.
A woman so beautiful, so pure, he would have done
anything for her.

And he did.

On a hunt for wild boar, separated from the main
group, he'd heard her shrill scream of terror and raced to
find her. Even terrified, she shone like a rose amidst the
brush. Pressed up against a tree trunk, her clothing torn
to reveal the tops of her creamy white breasts, her hair
speckled with leaves, her terror begged for a hero.
Without fear for his own safety, Xaphan had dashed into
the clearing to face the wild beast who gored her guard, a
dead idiot whose sword still rested in its sheath. Drawing
his with a metallic ring, Xaphan went head to head with
the creature, and won.

*Beast destroyed, adrenaline coursing through his veins, he
almost swung at the form hurtling at him. He held his hand at*

36

the last moment, recognizing his Lady. He didn't realize her intent until the she threw her arms around his armor clad torso and hugged him. Xaphan thought he would die on the spot so great was his shock – and pleasure.

"You saved me. How wondrous. And brave," she gushed, turning up a face shining with excitement.

Her slender form pressed tightly against him, Roxanne's creamy bosom so close he couldn't help but see the shadow of her cleavage. Words failed him, but despite her gratitude, he knew he needed to step away. Baseborn knights did not touch the daughters of their lords. And they most especially didn't lust after them, a fact his cock chose to ignore.

Xaphan drew back, but she didn't let him go entirely. Didn't give him the space he needed to regain his equilibrium. Roxanne clasped his hand and drew it to her breast. Pressed it against her softness as she continued to thank him in words that couldn't pierce the roaring in his ears. Under his calloused fingertips, digits that touched the swell of her bosom, her heart fluttered almost as quickly as his pounded.

The light brush of her lips over his, achieved by her standing on tip toe while he stood there frozen, was the moment he fell in love.

But he gained more that day than his Lord's thanks, and Roxanne's kiss of gratitude. Xaphan ended up reassigned as her personal bodyguard. He, a low, baseborn knight, ordered to stick to Roxanne's side, to protect her from all harm. An easy task, given his love for her, a love that eventually led him to deal with the Devil that he might save her. An unnecessary deal given that unbeknownst to him, Lucifer already had his eye on Xaphan, the half demon heritage he'd inherited from his father making him a prime soldier for his Lord's army.

Destiny decided despite his actions, he cashed in on the terms of his contract, killed for his lady, and descended to the pit, to serve the Devil. However, even surrounded by decadence, and temptation, he never let himself forget his one true love. His beautiful Roxanne.

"Forgive me my love for allowing impure thoughts of another to taint what we had. I will not allow her to take your place. No woman ever shall. Even in death, I belong only to you." He said the words, words he'd repeated a thousand times already to her image, the only thing left of her he owned. But even as he spoke the promise by rote, he couldn't completely erase the memory of a blue and green pair of eyes, and the perky warmth residing there. Didn't feel the usual misery and peace that came from keeping a promise to a woman who resided with the angels.

Cursing, he jumped to his feet and headed to his bedroom. *This is all that psycho female's fault.* Before he'd met her, he'd found it easy to ignore the slags that constantly propositioned him. None could ever match the beauty and purity of his Roxanne. And yet, Katie, with her plump figure, her mismatched gaze, her dirty, dirty – and oh so luscious – mouth managed to do so almost instantly. A spell. Madness. A reason had to exist for his mental turmoil – and arousal. But he didn't have time to visit a witch or a head shrink. Not if he wanted to steer clear of the giggling blonde psycho.

Strapping knives on his body, more than his usual arsenal, he prepared. A knapsack for clothes. Another for some basic supplies like food and water. He tossed things at random in the canvas bags, hurrying even though Katie didn't expect to meet him for several hours, a meeting he didn't intend to keep.

Yes, he'd lied. His Lord probably beamed in pride. Despite Lucifer's wishes, Xaphan couldn't work with the female. Didn't trust himself to. So, while she slept or tortured small animals, oblivious to his plan, he'd sneak back to the tunnel and follow it to the end into the swamp, or so she claimed citing sources she had in the palace.

Didn't matter. No matter where he exited, he'd do his best to block the entrance to keep her from following. He'd find the dragon, bring it back, and rid himself of the female his Lord thought to saddle him with.

He should have known it wouldn't be so easy.

Avoiding the beings populating the streets and his Lord's castle proved easy for someone like him whose very birthright instilled a stealth most couldn't hope to achieve. As a boy, his mother dead in childbirth, his father unknown, he'd blamed his skill for hiding on his need for self-preservation. Bastards without parents tended to earn the most cuffs. If they could catch you. With his special gift, it didn't happen often. Years later, he discovered he owed his ability to hide in shadows to his father, a demon long dead, who'd seduced his poor mother and left her to birth alone, a child with a heritage not meant for the mortal plane.

Half-human, half-darkness, he'd not come into his true heritage until he learned under the tutelage of a scarred, veteran in his Lord's army. The paltry skills he discovered as a child? A mere precursor to what he could truly do. It took years of bruises and broken bones before he learned to hide his tracks, to use the shadows as a weapon and a shield. His teacher didn't believe in mollycoddling and used each injury as a lesson. Xaphan learned quickly. His first victory – which earned him a promotion – resulted in the killing of his teacher, who smiled through blood covered teeth, and muttered, "About fucking time."

Sometimes he missed the ornery old bastard. Not for long.

Forget the past though. He had a dragon to find, and a psycho to avoid.

In utter silence, and cloaked in darkness, he returned to the garden and the stone which hid the tunnel. Locating the camouflaged lever, he pressed it, wincing at the grinding noise that seemed to echo so loudly. But he heard no answering footsteps or cries of alarm. No vexing female voice asking him what he did – although a twinge of guilt assailed him. It didn't stop him. Besides, it wasn't as if someone as mentally unbalanced as her would care if he left without her. Or so he told himself.

Slipping into the gloomy interior of the passage, he let his hands run over the smooth stone until he found a slight edge. Applying pressure, his search rewarded him as the portal slid shut, cutting off all the remaining light. But the darkness ever was his friend.

Eyesight adjusting to the black void, he jogged down the tunnel, past the point where he'd given Katie his coat, further and further still, the only sound accompanying him that of his breath and beating heart.

It took him almost two hours to make his way to the end where another boulder blocked the exit. He quickly found the latch to release it and soon exited into a moist jungle.

Taking a step out, he scanned the area quickly, noting the grey limbed trees with their heavy, hanging foliage, the soggy ground, the whining of large bugs, and the absence of two legged life. Heaving a sigh of relief, because for some odd reason he'd expected to have Katie pop up out of nowhere, he turned and found the mechanism to shut the door. With a whir and click, the stone slid shut, and to prevent it from opening, he grabbed a rock and despite the loud ruckus, whacked at the switch until it cracked. Satisfied no one would follow, he turned, and yelled.

"What the fuck!"

"Surprise," said Katie with a wave and a bright grin from her perch on a branch.

OKAY, SO IT WAS A LITTLE NAUGHTY OF HER TO HIDE HER presence while he set about making sure she couldn't follow. But really, despite her blonde hair – all natural and she owned the bush to prove it – she wasn't dumb. A gut feeling told her Xaphan would try and ditch her. So quicker than a succubus in a room full of naked men on Viagra could get off, she'd changed into more appropriate clothes, grabbed a few items, and scooted back to the tunnel.

A good thing she ran too because she only arrived about thirty minutes before him. And boy oh boy, did he appear mad, a sexy look for him.

"What are you doing here?" he growled.

Driving you crazy? Hmm, perhaps not the best answer with that vein throbbing in his forehead. In an attempt to curb her tongue, for the moment at least, she took a moment to admire his attire. Dressed in a black tank top that fit him like a second skin – and displayed arms bulging with muscle, yum – he'd ditched the leather pants for cargo ones with a ton of pockets, and dear Lucifer in Hell, he even wore a bandanna. How did he know she had a thing for Rambo?

"Hello, grumpy. You don't look happy to see me."

"I'm not."

For some reason, his answer dampened her spirit. "Now that's not nice. And here I thought you'd be happy I brought your coat back." She grabbed the jacket from the branch where she'd draped it and flung it at him.

He caught it and muttered a gruff, "Thanks." Dropping his bag, he opened it to stuff the jacket in.

"No problem, partner." She thought it best not to mention the pink rhinestones she'd added to the collar and cuffs while she waited. It would make a nice surprise for later. "So, are you going to explain why you were trying to abandon me?"

"No."

"Oh come on. Is it because I'm such a sweet and dainty thing, you wanted to spare me the grueling trek?"

"No."

"Because you wanted all the glory to yourself?"

"There's no glory in finding a pink dragon. Not for me at any rate."

"Ooh, then it must be a jealous wife or girlfriend, someone who can't handle the fact you're working with such a hottie."

"No." He said it quickly, but something in the way he looked away and his body stiffened told her she'd hit upon the truth. Tall, dark and grouchy was taken. Well that sucked. But at least it explained how he managed to repel her advances. Not that he would forever. All males, even the happy ones gave in to their darker desires eventually.

Okay, maybe not all. A few did manage to escape her like Lucifer, and Charon, oh and her friend Ysabel's mate, Remy. Actually, he'd always avoided her because of her reputation. He was one of the few smart ones. Most ignored the black widow rumors and made a play. Then died.

"Now that we're both here," she said brightly, "Where to first?"

"That will depend on the tracks," he replied kneeling on the spongy ground.

"Oh, if you're going to be scientific about it, then they went that way," she said pointing.

"And what are you basing that on? Feminine instinct? Because there's pretty flowers that way?"

"No silly, although those are good reasons. I'm afraid this has more to do with glaring evidence."

"Such as?"

Hopping from the branch, she snagged her hidden pack and slung it onto her back. "Because I took a peek around when I arrived and the only footprints from this hillock go that way."

"How can we be sure they're from our kidnapper?"

"The poor baby dragon lost a shiny scale on that nasty bush over there. They didn't bother hiding their tracks, and because there's water in every other direction. Any more questions, suspicious one?"

"My name is Xaphan."

43

"I know, but that's much too attractive a name to waste on such a grumpy pants demon."

"You're really annoying."

"Thank you," she said with a wide smile as she led the way with a wiggle. "It's my second most endearing quality."

"I'm afraid to ask what's your first."

"My lack of morals."

"Why am I not surprised," he mumbled.

"What about you? What's your best quality, other than the fact you frown like a champion?"

"Must we talk?"

"No. We could always skip that part and go straight to fucking."

His indrawn breath from behind her made her lips curl in delight. Despite himself, someone was interested.

"My best quality is probably loyalty. Once I make a promise, I don't break it. Ever."

She didn't miss his emphasis and could guess at his meaning. "So who's the lucky girl?"

"No one you've ever met. And never will."

"What? Are you telling me once we complete our mission I won't be invited to a family barbecue to meet the ball and chain and your little rug rats? How rude." Especially since she wanted to see the paragon who'd managed to snare Mr. Serious.

"I have no children."

His use of 'I' was interesting. So of course, she couldn't let it go. "I? Doesn't your wife have a say?"

A heavy sigh left him. "Must you keep prying?"

"Yes. Or have you changed your mind about the sex?"

"Suffice it to say, children aren't in my future."

Again, she got the impression of some deeper meaning, but she couldn't figure it out this time. Was his wife barren? Did he have slow swimmers? Bored by cryptic answers, and somewhat annoyed by the woman he seemed determined to keep a mystery, she changed the subject.

"So I called my source about the tunnel and she told me that only a handful of people and demons know about it. I've got a friend looking into the whereabouts of the names she gave me."

"And just how can you know this source is reliable and not lying?"

"Given Muriel avoids lying just to piss off her dad, I'd say it's pretty accurate."

"Muriel, as in Lucifer's daughter?"

"The one and only. It's her baby girl's pet dragon missing. Not that Muriel's all that heartbroken about it. She told her dad Lucinda was too young for the responsibility of a pet. But Lucifer spoils the little girl."

"Let's back up a second. Muriel gave you a list of the names she thinks know about the tunnel. But, we can't be sure who those people told, or even if our Lord told others about it."

"And, don't forget smart people like me who might have stumbled across it."

She ignored his snort at the word smart. But she'd remember later when she carved a body part off.

"So anyone could have known about the tunnel. A better question is why? Why take a pink dragon knowing the Devil is going to want it back? It's not like they can easily sell it. Anyone who sees it will know who it belongs to."

Katie rolled her shoulders in a shrug. "Why do beings do any of the things they do? Because they can. Because they're greedy. And because they think no one will stop them. My job is to teach them otherwise." Her statement came out sounding darker and more menacing than she meant, and she could feel his gaze boring into her back as he digested it. Oops, she'd almost slipped. "Oh, look at the pretty flower." Bending over, she drew his attention to the way her jeans molded to her bottom. When she straightened, she smiled as she watched him marching, stiff as a board past her.

Already she could see the cracks in his resolve. She just needed to apply more pressure.

4

DESPITE HER DITZY EXTERIOR, Katie proved tougher than he would have wagered. Though they slogged for hours through the marsh, fought the mud sucking at their boots, slapped away insects of a ridiculous size, which kept swooping in looking for a taste, and the stench suffocating them in a miasma more vile than a barrack full of demons after a grueling fifteen mile jog, she didn't utter one word of complaint. But that was the only thing she didn't remark on. The woman never shut up.

"Ooh, look at that stump. Doesn't it look like Grikle? Do you know him? He works as the bouncer at that club in the third ring. What's the name of the place again? Oh yeah, Dance Your Balls Off. Do you know he..."

On and on it went. An endless prattle that should have driven him mad, made him roll his eyes at the very least, but instead, he learned a great many things about the denizens of Hell. Most of it useless, but what fascinated him was not only her memory but the observations she made. Despite her airhead exterior, Katie possessed a sharp mind that noted everything around her, even the most miniscule item. It seemed at odds with her personality.

If someone were to torture him, he might have even admitted, to himself only, how he also enjoyed how capable she seemed as they trekked. Unlike a certain lady he used to know – and still loved – she didn't require him to carry her over puddles, even when they swirled menacingly as the denizens showed interest in their passage. She didn't cry when a bird flew over and dropped a steaming pile on her shoulder. Sluicing it off, she claimed it was good luck and kept going. Hell, she didn't even flinch when the snake – thicker than her thigh – tried to wind itself around her calf. Without even pausing in her recital of restaurants she enjoyed, she clubbed it on the head hard enough to make the serpent drop and slither away, as fast as it could go.

Damn, but she fascinated him, and with nothing but endless views of grey, brown and soggy marsh to look at, he couldn't help but focus on her – and wish he'd taken a minute to jerk off before coming. Fuck did he have the sorest balls imaginable.

"We should stop," she suddenly announced when they climbed up onto a hillock that, while damp, provided firm footing.

"Good idea. We could both use a drink to stay hydrated."

"Drink? Who has time for that? I need to fix my poor nail." To his disbelief, she whipped out a bottle of bright pink nail polish and proceeded to dab at her chipped enamel.

"Unfucking believable," he said shaking his head.

"Tell me about it. The salon promised me that the hard coat could withstand everyday use. Someone's head will roll for this."

She threatened with a smile, and yet, he got the funny feeling she wasn't entirely kidding. Even odder, she reminded him of himself when the tailor fucked up his alterations. He had removed his head. Bounced it a few times, then had it reattached. The soul survived. A little traumatized, but he never messed up his pants again.

Chewing on a piece of jerky, Xaphan watched her as she admired her handiwork. "How do you know the swamp so well?"

"Because I love the mud baths. Naked of course. When I'm feeling stressed, or in need of some me time, I come out to Hell's own bayou, strip down, sink into the ooey, gooey muck and let it cover my bare body." She skimmed her hands down her body and smiled at him coyly.

A fluffy answer and cock hardening image, but he didn't believe it. "Great cover, but now how about giving me the real reason?"

She opened her eyes wide, trying to appear innocent, as if she could manage that with those full – perfect for cocksucking – lips. "What makes you think I'm lying?"

"I didn't say you were. I do believe you enjoy immersing yourself in the mud, but I think your knowledge of the swamp arises from a different reason. Tell me. Or are you chicken?" Why he taunted her, he couldn't have said, but oddly, he wanted to know more about her. What hid behind the laughter and insane sexual innuendos she kept tossing his way? He'd castigate himself for the reason why later.

"Ooh a dare. I like it. Maybe there is hope for you after

all, grumpy. Fine. You've brow beaten me into it, although, I would have preferred a spanking. You're right. I don't just come to the swamp for the mud baths, or moonshine, even if the stuff is damned good. I come here, on an almost weekly basis because it's the number one spot for fugitives."

His brow creased. "Fugitives from what?"

She rolled her eyes. "Hell of course. You of all people should know that the demons in this place don't always toe the line. And when some of those idiots cross it, then punishment, also known as me, is their reward. Of course, most can't handle the repercussions to their crime, that or they're so awed by the concept of meeting me, that they run, and for some reason, it's almost always to the swamp."

"And you're the one who fetches them back?"

A smile tilted her lips. "Parts of them at any rate. Lucifer only sends me after the ones he doesn't want back alive."

"You're an executioner?" He sounded incredulous.

She nodded her head.

"How come I've never heard of you?"

"Like duh, because my targets are dead of course."

And then he did the worst thing possible, or so he assumed a moment later. He laughed.

IT SEEMED SHE'D DONE HER JOB OF CONVINCING XAPHAN she was a harmless girl a little too well. When she gave him the truth, because he demanded it, he actually had the nerve to laugh. At her!

Boy, did that rate high on her list of things not to do, right after touching her New York style cheesecake. Faster than a succubus could drop to her knees for a bared cock, she pinned him, her lithe body flying through the air, tumbling him backwards. Sitting high up on his chest, her legs pinning his arms, a pair of knives held at his throat, she grinned down at him.

"Still think I'm lying?"

"No. And I can see why I've never heard of you. Who'd want to admit they got taken down by a girl?"

"You forgot to add super sexy in front of that. It's a good thing I like you, grumpy, or you'd be dead."

And he still didn't take her seriously.

Did Xaphan not understand his vulnerable position? By what tiny thread he held onto life? Apparently not, that or he was slightly mad – *just like me, hehehe* – because he continued to laugh. She liked it. The rumble of it, low and sexy, not only vibrated her crotch where it rested on his chest, it enveloped her in a warmth that made her brow knit in confusion. Since when did she allow a male, or anyone for that matter, to laugh at her? She needed to reassert control.

"Do you have a death wish?"

"No."

"A fetish for knives?"

"No."

"Then I fail to see, demon, just what you think is so funny. It's also starting to piss me off." She pressed the points of her knife deeper, dimpling his skin. With a wink, she would have never suspected him capable of, he wavered beneath her, his entire presence blurring and distorting. Then, he disappeared.

Hitting the ground, she quickly recovered, crouching and peering around her. *Where did he go?*

She never heard him approach or reappear. All of a sudden, two arms came out of nowhere to pin her hands at her side.

"How did you do that?" she exclaimed, more surprised than annoyed that he'd managed to fool her.

"You're not the only one with a skill our Lord finds useful," he murmured close to her ear.

"You can turn invisible? Cool." *I am so jealous.*

His soft chuckle tickled across the skin of her neck and she shivered. Craning her head back, she looked at him, and met a gaze burning with heat.

"I can do a lot of things," he said in a husky whisper.

"A man of many talents. There's more to you than meets the eye, demon." In their position, their mouths were so close. How easily she could –

"Duck!" she yelled as she suddenly recalled where she was and what the bubbling noise behind them meant.

Throwing her down, Xaphan covered her body with his own seconds before the swamp exploded with a wet 'Pop!' Something went flying over them, sprinkling them with muddy drops.

"What the fuck was that?" he asked.

Stunned he'd use his own body to protect her, she took a second to answer. "Flying mud toad. They take down their prey by launching themselves from the muck, latching on with razor sharp teeth and injecting their victim with a paralyzing agent. Then, after calling some friends, they nibble you apart and drag you back to their home."

"How do they taste?" was his surprising question.

Even though he still lay atop her, a heavy, hard male-ness that didn't intimidate her as expected, she smiled. "Excellent when roasted over a fire with some herbs."

"I brought salt, pepper and garlic."

"And I'm hungry."

An hour later, the aroma of a crispy toad, roasted to perfection, filled the air. "Dinner time," she sang.

Turning from the lean to he'd constructed out of vines and wood – the second one, since he apparently had no intention of sharing the first one he built – Xaphan nodded his head, his grim expression back.

Despite his earlier laughter and joking, he'd quickly returned to the somber demon she'd come to know. A shame, because while handsome when grumpy, he proved devastating when he smiled. But she'd somehow ruined it, broken her fun demon when she'd wiggled her bottom under him and asked him if he intended to do her doggy style. Erection pressing against her bottom or not, he'd jumped off her like she carried the plague, and not come near her since.

She could almost admire his determination to keep himself at arm's-length. Only...*I want him.* Boy, did she ever. The vile groping she put up with while growing up might have made her leery of all men, and turned her into an awesome killer, but that didn't mean she didn't end up with a healthy sexual appetite. She had needs. Needs she liked to feed. And when she finished scratching that itch, and realized she'd made herself vulnerable, well, she just killed the problem.

Of course, she'd never attempted that before with a demon of Xaphan's caliber. She usually stuck to males she knew she could easily overpower. Demons who never even suspected they had it coming. Would she manage the same with her grumpy partner?

Hopefully she'd have the answer by the time she finished with him.

XAPHAN COULD SENSE HER WATCHING HIM. HE DIDN'T EVEN need to turn to know she did. He felt it. And hated it.

For a moment, he'd let the rigid strictures he'd placed on himself loosen. He'd laughed with a woman. Smiled for her and because of her. Covered her with his body when he thought danger imminent. Oh sweet hell, he'd not counted on enjoying having her under him so much, her body a perfect fit against his. Then she'd asked him to take her, on her hands and knees. He almost did. He could even see it in his mind; her rounded body propped up, her plentiful buttocks spread to accommodate his cock sinking into her, his hands gripping those cheeks as he slammed into her warm, wet sheath.

Despite the possibility of another flying toad, he jumped to his feet and put some distance between them. Damn her for the hurt that came into her eyes, a pain she quickly masked as she rose with a smile and a promise to return in a minute with dinner.

Trusting her supposed expertise, he set himself the task of building a shelter, while keeping an eye on her as she waded in the bog and stood, still as a statue. He let his hands weave the vines by rote as he kept silent sentry to her hunt, prepared to dive at a moment's notice to save her if needed. But, his psycho partner – and tempting vixen – truly hid more inside than just a sharp mind. When the toad flew up – a slimy looking critter with bulging eyes, gangly limbs and razor sharp teeth

– it didn't even have time to croak before she impaled it on a knife. He could only watch in amazement – and grudging admiration – as she dispatched with a grace that stole his breath, the vengeful critters as they boiled from the depths. *Damn, she's fast.* And definitely not squeamish.

Keeping only the largest ones, she yakked away as she gutted, spitted, seasoned and then cooked the toads. Xaphan didn't reply to her chatter, which he began to suspect she used to disarm and fool those around her into thinking her stupid, and nonthreatening.

She's threatening alright. Just not in a knife in the heart kind of way. Somehow, someway, she was worming her way under the shield he'd erected to guard his emotions. She'd already smashed through the restraint he held over his lust, making her so dangerous. Could he truly resist her if she put her mind to seducing him? Did he want to?

No dammit. I made a vow. A vow she tested with every giggle and smirk.

Knowing his weakness kept growing the more time he spent around her, he decided it prudent to build a second lean-to, fearful of what might happen if he slept so close to her side. Although she never said a word about his actions, despite all the speech that spewed forth from her perfect lips, he could see the amusement in her eyes.

Sitting down for dinner, on the opposite side of the fire, he grabbed a spit with a golden roasted critter and prepared to eat. Katie sat across from him, legs in a lotus position, which he found quite intriguing given the tightness of her jeans.

EVE LANGLAIS

Tugging a piece of meat from his portion, he chewed with pleasure. "This is good," he said, surprised.

"Not as good as my pie."

Choking, he grabbed the bottle of water she tossed at him. "Would you stop doing that?" he growled when he got his breath back – although he couldn't dispel the image of himself between her thighs eating said pie.

"Doing what?" she asked, innocence personified.

"Making everything into some kind of sexual come on."

"What? Because I said my pie is good. It really is, you know? Tasty. Hot. Filling. Moist. And with the lightest crust in all the nine circles of Hell, or so I've been told."

"Pie? As in the kind you bake?" he asked faintly.

"My cherry is a favorite." And yes, she managed to say that with a straight face.

He wanted to beat his head on the ground. "I swear you do this on purpose."

"Do what?"

"Nothing." No way was he admitting she got him hotter than the fires of Hell. Or that every time she opened her mouth, he longed to fill it with something.

"Maybe you can have a taste of my pie when we finish here in the swamp." The lick of her lips and the twinkle in her mismatched eyes had him shaking his head.

"What am I going to do with you?"

"I can think of lots of things, but you keep saying no. Is she that special, this woman of yours?"

Who? Oh, Roxanne. Faced with Katie and her beguiling presence, he couldn't even picture his one true love in his mind. But he knew the answer to the question at least. "Very."

"She's one lucky lady then." The compliment emerged wistfully, and he shot a look only to see Katie peering at the marsh, chewing on her supper.

"Do you have a mate?" A burning curiosity made him ask. Not that he cared. Really he didn't, even if he listened avidly for her answer.

"I don't believe in relationships."

"But you apparently believe in sex."

She smiled. "Sex is a bodily need. Waking up next to someone and having them try to give you orders because of a hole between your legs isn't."

"That sounds pretty harsh."

"Oh please. Most males love the fact I don't want a relationship. Just hot, sweaty sex."

"There's a name for girls like that." Annoyed at her boast, but not understanding why, he insulted her.

"Awesome comes to mind. Anything else will get you killed," she said with smirk.

The conversation at a dead end, he avoided replying by taking a drink and eating some more of his roasted toad. It didn't take long for her to ruin the silence.

"So you seem kind of handy out here for a guy who doesn't know squat about the marsh."

"What makes you think I don't know anything about bogs?"

"Oh please. Let's start with the obvious. Shit kicking boots that fill with water unlike my super water slippers." She pointed her toes in the form fitting pink shells that even outlined her toes. "You brought bug spray when a bug bite out here is likely to kill you given its size. And, you'd never seen one of the flying toads before. They're like the first creature you learn about out here."

EVE LANGLAIS

"For your information, I wear these boots everywhere. But on the rest you're right, I don't know much about Hell's swamps. I spend most of my time on the mortal side. While you catch those who escape down here, I take care of those who think to cause havoc on the human plane. Since my prey doesn't always head for the nearest city and civilization, I've learned a few skills to keep me comfortable."

"I don't miss that world or the occupants at all," she stated. "I find demons much more honest in their dealings than humans."

"Honest?" He almost choked.

She shrugged. "They're very forthright about their intentions." She deepened her voice. "Hey blonde girl, I am going to you fuck into next week.' They give me all the excuses I need to end their lives."

He couldn't refute that. How many lives had he ended because a demon dared to look at him with an expression he didn't care for?

"What about the damned souls?" he asked.

"What about them?"

"You said you didn't miss the occupants of the mortal plane. Before their deaths, the damned were human, and given their massive population, it's not like you can avoid them around here."

"Ah, but unlike the living ones, they don't have the power to hurt me here." As if sensing the dark direction of their conversation, she smiled. "Gotta love Hell. I get to kill things without punishment. I prefer getting paid to do what I love than dancing to ten thousand volts."

"Excuse me?"

"Didn't Lucifer tell you? I was electrocuted for my

58

crimes. Not so great for the mortal body, but it gave my bush a wicked curl. The media called me Killer Katie. They credited me with thirteen deaths even though it was actually more. Idiots."

Bombarded with facts, one thing did make him frown. "If you died, then how did you avoid becoming a damned soul?"

"Lucifer owned my life well before I got caught, silly."

"I get that you made a deal. But I thought only witches got to keep their bodies when they got here. All other humans become damned souls unless they've made a deal. But, I've met some of those, and you're not like them."

"You mean, a fang wearing, blood sucking, sun allergic vampire? If I'd have known how Twilight was going to make their kind popular, I might have opted for that."

"Obviously you didn't. So how did you avoid becoming one of the undead?"

"Magic. Nefertiti, Lucifer's hot shot mage, did some fancy mumbo jumbo thing on me. It hurt worse than a knife in the gut, but I have to say the end result rocked. Not only did I get to keep my super awesome body, Lucifer even sent me back to have my vengeance."

The conversation fascinated him as she gave him answers without her usual giggles and innuendos. "Vengeance against whom?"

A dark smile twisted her lips. "Those even more evil than I."

"You don't seem that evil to me."

"That only shows how little you know. And trust me, it's best if you keep it that way."

Xaphan wanted to ask her more questions. She'd only told him enough to whet his curiosity, but she proceeded to do things with meat that would have sold tickets to even the most perverse. In order to fight an image of her doing the same to his hunk of meat, he ducked his head and ate.

The rest of their dinner passed in silence, and the time for bed arrived.

"Do we need to lay traps or take turns on watch?" He deferred to her since she seemed to know the place so well.

"Nah. The flying toads won't be coming back, not for a while at any rate, and seeing as how I scattered the remains around our little island to feed the other critters, we'll be safe enough. Or wake up with a foot chewed off. But that doesn't happen too often."

With those words of wisdom and a wink, she dove into a shelter with her pack. Xaphan didn't immediately move, instead stoking the fire, adding a wet piece of wood that threw up thick smoke. He knew he should rest. The marsh wasn't a place for weakness or fatigue. However, with his mind spinning, rest seemed impossible. Not with Katie so close.

Why now, after centuries, did he find himself so intrigued by a woman? While cute, she didn't possess Roxanne's ethereal beauty, although, he did admire Katie's more curvaceous figure. Katie was crude. A tease. Not afraid to get dirty. Fearless. And just as fucked up as him. Where that certainty came from, he couldn't have said. Something in her eyes perhaps. The way she regarded everyone with a wary eye hidden by her laughter. The hints she'd given of a troubled past, a past that led her to join Lucifer's ranks. He still wanted to know what she needed vengeance for.

However, it wasn't just curiosity about the enigma she presented that drew him. There was more to it than that. Perhaps he sensed her as a kindred spirit, one that was hurt in the past and made a promise to never allow it to happen again.

Feeling an affinity, however farfetched though, wasn't a reason to forsake his vows. He'd promised to never love another. *But what I'm feeling isn't love.* Far from it. Annoyance. Irritation. Frustration. Easy emotions to ignore. The one he couldn't seem to halt though was arousal.

Had his body decided to rebel against his celibate state? After so long did it frantically need the touch of a woman? What else to explain his insane attraction? And to a psycho?

Maybe if I fuck her, it will go away. But, the very act would betray the vow he made. A dilemma without a solution. *Unless I'm ready to let my love for Roxanne go.* The very thought of it seemed blasphemous – and so appealing. He'd held on to his misery for so long. Martyrdom for a love that he no longer even remembered. *I don't even recall how love feels. Did I ever feel it at all?*

During his time with Roxanne, a few short months, he remembered the worry over getting caught and the frantic nature of their few intimate moments together. Hell, he'd never even seen Roxanne fully undressed. Just skirts up around her waist while he quickly gave her what she demanded in breathy pants. They'd never really talked either. His awe of her made him silent. After all, what did he, a measly knight with no land or money have to say of worth?

When he did open his mouth it was usually to blurt another promise to always protect her. *My sword is yours, my lady.* She'd graciously accepted it. And used it, asking with her soft voice for him to kill those who wronged her. The number, in retrospect, was high.

But she loved me. And I loved her. His use of the past tense didn't escape him. Did he no longer love the woman he'd sold his life for? The woman who begged him to save her at the expense of his soul? The human half at any rate.

The foreign thoughts, betrayals in a sense, made him dig the heels of his hands into his eye sockets. This was Katie's fault. Damn that psycho with her bouncy walk and saucy smiles. She'd done something to him. Something to make him doubt his course. His existence. She –

A whimper froze him and he lifted his head to listen. What creature could mimic so well the forlorn cry of a female? Katie slept or he would have asked her. Craning to listen, he waited to see if it would repeat and from what direction.

But it wasn't an animal, and the sound occurred again right behind him. He turned to look at the lean-to Katie occupied.

"Katie?" He called her name softly, but she didn't answer. Creeping closer, he peered into the shelter. Nothing seemed amiss, and yet, he noted her lips trembled while her lashes fluttered.

She dreamed – and not something pleasant he'd wager by the way she twitched in her sleep. Did her actions haunt her? Did something frighten her? He debated waking her when she exploded in a flurry of movement, screaming, "I don' think so, mother fucker. Don't touch me. I'll kill you. I'll fucking kill you."

Xaphan jumped clear as she slashed with a pair of

gleaming daggers, eyes shut and unseeing, at some invisible monster.

"Katie." He tried to get her attention. "Katie." He spoke louder when she continued to curse and stab. Given her dangerous actions, he finally shouted, "Hey psycho! Wake up!"

That finally got through to her. A green and a blue eye opened and fixed on him. Madness shone in their depths mixed with the frightened ferocity of a wild animal backed into a corner. For some reason, her expression tightened his heart.

Before either could do or say anything, the lean-to collapsed on her.

STUPID NIGHTMARES. SHE'D HOPED ONCE SHE KILLED THOSE who hurt and betrayed her, they would stop. When they didn't, she'd killed some more, and more. But nothing could completely stop the night terrors from consuming her subconscious when she slept.

Bummer.

Most thought her madness – and anger issues – came to her naturally. Not so. Once upon a time, Katie was normal. Wearing pig tails and pinafores, she'd lived a happy dream of a life. Then her dad left, with barely a goodbye to the little girl who worshipped him, and her mom remarried.

Harry, the prick, didn't take long after the wedding to show his true colors. A drunken brute, he slapped her mother around, and when Katie tried to intervene, hit her too. But bruises healed, and she learned to avoid his alcoholic temper – especially when she spiked his favorite rum with laxatives. All that changed in her early tweens when he stumbled into her bedroom. As if she'd let him touch her. She'd screamed for her mother. Staggering in, wearing a tattered pink night robe, her mother took one look and shrugged. Then walked out.

But Harry, sobering enough from the incident, even with her mother's silent permission given, didn't stay. And after that, Katie slept with a knife. Not that he returned. Soon after, he left and another man came into her mother's life. He didn't even try to stem his lecherous thoughts. So Katie stabbed him. Hands covered in blood as he lay gasping on the floor, her mother entered and with a cry of horror dropped to her knees crying, "What have you done?"

So much for a mother's love and need to protect her child.

Betrayed, she killed the woman who birthed her, and not in the mood to wait for the cops, Katie left, becoming another waif on the streets. However, with freedom came vulnerability. Men and boys alike preyed on her. Wanted her to do things for money. She refused and fought off their advances. But their grasping hands and sloppy kisses frightened her, especially when they caught her unawares or in a group. How could she protect herself?

She prayed to God. Prayed until her knees bled. That prick never answered other than to send more misery her way. Pissed, and at the end of her rope, she called to another Lord, the dark one.

Lucifer arrived in a swirl of smoke that had her waving it away just to take a breath. When it cleared, a benign male in a suit stood before her, a quill in one hand, a handwritten scroll in the other.

"Will you help me?" she asked, eyes narrowed in suspicion.

"I will." Over a dinner he conjured with a snap of his fingers, they hammered out their deal. And Katie never regretted it.

Now if only the nightmares of those times before, the moments when she was a helpless little girl, would stop. Her first shrink said in order to stop them, she needed to recognize not all men were assholes. She threw his ass in the abyss. Her next shrink gave her pills. When those didn't work, she also threw his ass in the abyss. Her third shrink, who would only deal with her by phone, told her that she was like a princess under a curse. Kind of like sleeping beauty, a damsel in distress who needed to fall in love, except in her case, instead of waking up, love would banish the night terrors.

The concept intrigued her. She'd always liked fairytales, but there was just one problem. She kept killing her possible suitors. She couldn't help herself. They got close. She panicked. And oops, there went another pair of white running shoes.

But really, the nightmares weren't that bad, even if they wreaked havoc on her sheets and mattress. Or in this case, a lean-to.

Lying amidst the debris of her shelter, she allowed herself to calm down as the demon pulled the branches off her, cursing as he worked. Revealed a moment later, she noted the concern in Xaphan's face. How long since she'd seen a man wear an expression like that for her? *Did anyone in my life before I came here, ever care?*

"Are you okay?" he asked, offering her a hand. She gripped it and he used his strength to heave her from the wreckage. Other than a few scratches, she emerged essentially unscathed. Well, so long as you didn't count her mental state. But that broke a long time ago.

"I'm fine. Nothing a few kisses won't fix." She puckered up, but he didn't take advantage.

"I see your sense of humor survived," he remarked dryly, spinning her to check her back.

"Life's not worth living if you can't laugh."

He didn't reply.

"Sorry, if I woke you."

"I wasn't sleeping yet."

"Well, I intend to. A girl needs her beauty rest." Snagging her pack from the pile of sticks, she tossed it beside the fire, and lay down, pillowing her head on its canvas surface.

"Take my shelter."

Damn, but the demon had a chivalrous streak a mile wide. It annoyed her. She didn't need him treating her like a girl. "I'm fine. Really. Nothing like a night sleeping out in the open."

Even though she had her back to him, she could sense him staring at her. With a sigh, he moved and the sound of him crawling into the intact lean-to made her relax. What a jerk, though, acting all nice and gentlemanly. She didn't need him messing up the perceptions she'd built over the years about males – selfish, mean and deserving of death creatures.

Let him keep his shelter. I'm going to sleep out here by the fire, enjoying the cloudy night sky and the softly drifting ash. And the rain which taunted her with soft wet splatters.

Shaking a fist at the sky, she didn't even bother to argue when he growled, "Get in here."

Throwing her pack in first, she crawled into the tight space. "Hey roomie." She snuggled in alongside him, the lean-to just barely wide enough for them both, and only if they lay on their sides. Wet and cold away from the fire – the heat of Hell not warm enough to thaw her cold heart – she couldn't help shivering.

A heavy arm snaked around her middle and dragged her close. Xaphan pulled her until she was flush with his frame, her back against his chest, her butt snuggled into his groin. Spooning. Now there was something she'd never done. It was pleasant. Warm. Comforting. Not something she trusted at all.

"So was this all part of your master plan to get me to sleep with you?" she teased.

"Yes because I have the ability to call rain on demand," he replied, not bothering to stem his sarcasm. "Since we're both awake, care to tell me what the nightmare was about?"

"What nightmare? I don't know what you're talking about."

"Of course you don't." He shifted behind her, inching his groin away. It didn't take a genius to figure out why.

"Someone seems a little tense. I know what would fix that." In case her innuendo wasn't clear, she wiggled her bottom against him. Bingo. Someone definitely sported an erection.

"Don't do that." He inched back.

"What?" She shimmied closer.

"I said no."

"Why? Your wife isn't here. I won't tell."

"But I'll know."

"And that matters to you?"

"Yes. I made a promise and I intend to keep it."

The concept intrigued her. What would it be like to have someone who loved her that much? Who would make a vow to her and actually mean it? Problem was, he'd not made that vow to her, so she felt no need to heed it. "Come on. Give me something. I'm too wound up to sleep."

"No."

"Then how about I give you something? We can have our very own Lewinsky moment."

"No."

"A kiss? Surely, one itty bitty kiss wouldn't hurt."

"Will you shut up and go to sleep if I do?"

Surprise engulfed her at his agreement. "Cross my heart."

"Fine."

Oh, but how she loved it when he used his growly voice. Rolling to her back, she could only see the glow of his eyes as he hovered over her. She reached a hand up, not even thinking, and cupped his bristled cheek. As if that were a signal, he swooped in. She could tell he meant to give her a quick peck and retreat. But she wasn't about to let him get off that easily. Not when she'd imagined this kiss for hours at this point.

Both of her hands snaked around his neck and locked him into place as his lips touched hers. When he would have drawn back, she held tight and moved her mouth over his. He tried to resist. Kept his lips clamped shut, his body rigid. But she didn't relent, sliding her lips over his until a groan escaped him, and his passion unleashed.

Holy hell. The demon could kiss.

Hot, panting and oh so fierce, he claimed her mouth, spread it open for the assault of his tongue, which claimed hers, caressed it. Need swept through her. Wetness pooled in her sex like she'd never imagined. Her nipples pearled. And all because of his kiss.

What an embrace. He devoured her as if starving. Sucked on her lower lip, tongue... Their breaths mingled, to the point the soft sounds of pleasure could have been hers, or his. A heavy thigh inserted itself between hers, pressing against her core, and she arched, rubbing herself against him like a succubus in heat.

More, she wanted more. She wanted to tear his clothes off. To feel him, skin to skin. To have him cover her body as he thrust into her.

The sizzling arousal, so strong, so overwhelming, frightened her. She felt bemused. Unable to stop the waves of passion he incited. He commanded the moment and her body. Things spun quickly out of control. The realization brought back her sanity.

She pulled away from his kiss, even though she never wanted to stop. She braced her palms on his shoulders and held him back – even if she wanted to remain crushed against him – and opened her eyes to see his glittering down at her, the confusion – and arousal – in them clear.

She'd asked for it. Teased him for it. And boy, had he given it to her. So what was a girl to say when she'd gotten him all riled up with no intention of going any further? "Thanks for the kiss. See you in the morning."

His eyebrows shot up.

With her heart still pounding, her body throbbing and

aching, every nerve ending singing, she rolled onto her side, her back to him. She said not a word as he once again draped his arm over her. Didn't utter a peep, didn't wiggle a bit even though she could actually hear his heart beating just as erratically.

She didn't dare do a single thing, because if she did, if they took up where that one kiss left off, she wouldn't stop. She'd ride him until she screamed in orgasm. And while she'd enjoy it, she wasn't ready to kill him yet.

5

After the worst night of sleep ever – sore balls, a rock hard cock, a baffled mind and a sexy snorer snuggled at his side did not make for a good night's sleep – they packed up their things and took off again in the morning. Xaphan stayed silent while Katie babbled nonstop, seemingly unaffected by the kiss they shared. A kiss he couldn't forget. A kiss he wanted to repeat. An embrace that had him reassessing his life. Because there was one thing he couldn't deny, what he'd shared with Roxanne never came close to the passion that consumed him when touching Katie.

"Hell to grumpy demon. Hell calling. Do you read me?"

Snapped out of his thoughts – that circled endlessly without a solution, or one he approved of at any rate – he chastised himself for not paying better attention. Anything could have attacked them. Judging by the slime on Katie's arm, something did, and instead of acting like a veteran soldier, he'd mooned over a kiss.

Straightening his spine, placing his hand on his sword

hilt, he promised himself to do better, especially since
they approached some primitive type of village in the
midst of the marsh.

"Where the fuck are we?" he asked. He eyed with
disgust the wattle huts held together, if his nose wasn't
mistaken, by mud and shit.

"Swamptown."

"Seriously?" Originality at its finest.

"Yes, and don't say anything about it unless you want
to take on the whole town. They're kind of touchy about
the subject."

"Simpletons usually are," he muttered.

The smile she flashed him made his heart beat faster.
"You are so judgmental. Have I mentioned I like it?"

"Because you're whacked." He uttered the rebuke
almost fondly, and she grinned wider. "I take it by your
knowledge of this cesspool's name that you've been here
before?"

"Yup. It's the only real town of note in the marshes,
mostly because it's on high enough ground to not get
swept away when the storms hit. Fugitives often end up
here, hence my familiarity. And even when I'm not hunting, I pop in for the occasional visit, using the main path
of course, not the route we took."

"Why the fuck would you come here to visit?" The
squalor and inhabitants alone would make a sane person
shy away. Oops, answered his own question.

"I love the mud baths remember?"

At his incredulous look she laughed. "Okay, and the
moonshine. You haven't drunk anything until you've
choked down some good ol' fashioned, liquid, bayou fire."

"No thanks."

"You don't know what you're missing, grumpy. Maybe when we're done here, I'll bring you back and buy you a drink. Loosen you up a bit."

"Over my dead body."

"Ooh, I accept your challenge."

"That was not a challenge."

"Sure it wasn't." She rolled her eyes in an expression that claimed he lied.

"You're nuts."

"And you're repetitive. Now, I know you're eager for me to lead you into temptation, else you wouldn't be constantly daring me, but we need to focus on work first."

"I am doing no such thing."

A slow wink went with her, "Sure, you're not. You keep telling yourself that, big guy. Ooh!" She clapped her hands. "I just found a clue. Judging by that collar hanging over in that stall, this is where our kidnapper brought the dragon."

Sure enough, the golden ring, engraved with the word 'Fluffy,' glinted in the feeble light spilling from the ash clouds. A squat demon, his green skin covered in pustules, one eye hidden by a dirty patch, with tusks, yellow sharp spikes that jutted from the side of his mouth, saw them looking and spat.

"Piece of jewelry for your slut?"

Placing one hand on her hip and eyeing Xaphan up and down, Katie bit her lower lip and cocked her head. "I don't know. After all those steroids, he's got a rather thick neck for that bauble. Could you make me one a tad bit smaller? Not too small. Lucky for me, his neck isn't the only thing that's big." She giggled as she said it.

Torn between a desire to puff up at her praise, and

hide because she'd said it to a stranger, instead, Xaphan focused on the vendor, whose leer really begged to get acquainted with his fist.

"I can't make you another, blondie. This here one was gotten on a trade."

A pout didn't make her any less cute. "Oh phooey. I don't suppose you know who gave it to you. Maybe I can find him and ask him if he can make another."

Single eye narrowing in suspicion, the vendor hawked a loogie to the side. "Nope. Don't recall."

"What a shame," she said, leaning forward.

Having been the recipient of that move and the abundant amount of cleavage it displayed, Xaphan could understand the glazed look and drool hanging from the seller's mouth. He didn't like it though, both the drool and the fact someone else looked at her with less than pristine thoughts.

"I would be ever so grateful," she purred, "if you could remember." She dragged a finger down the stained tunic of the demon.

"Uh. Uh." Shivering and sweating, the vendor could only look at her and stutter.

A frown knitting her forehead, she leaned back. "Darn it. I forgot the demons out here never get any. He's going to be useless to me now until the blood returns to his brain."

"Touch me and I'll tell you anything you want," the demon managed to blurt before cupping himself.

"Like fuck," Xaphan growled. His sword sang, a metallic clarion that stopped the voices in the dirty street. He held the point of it against the demon's throat. "Tell the lady what she wants to know or I'll slice off pieces, starting with the part you're currently thinking with."

"You can't threaten me," the dirty demon blubbered.

"Says who?"

"Says us," warbled a wet sounding voice.

Keeping his sword at the demon's throat, Xaphan turned his head and saw the crowd of disreputable demons, damned souls and other beings, encroaching his space.

"I am here on the Lord's business. So stand aside." Back braced with pride, his voice rang out loud and clear, without a hint of fear. She had to admire his steadfast courage, even if it would get him killed.

"Or else what?" spat a troll with a gut that hung low over his loin cloth.

"Katie, please watch our informant while I teach the scum in this town to respect their Lord and his minions."

"Ooh. A fight!" she squealed. "Ten liters of granny's moonshine says Xaphan kicks your arses back into the swamp."

"Only ten?" Xaphan replied with a ghost of a smile as he drew his sword to his side and rolled his shoulders in preparation.

"What was I thinking? One hundred liters."

With his psycho cheering him on – something he admittedly enjoyed – Xaphan melted with the shadows, and every time he stepped forth, a resident of Swamp-town died, or in the cases of the damned who couldn't, lay in pieces.

CLAPPING HER HANDS IN GLEE, KATIE SAT ON THE VENDORS table and watched. Behind her, the demon with bad breath cheered his friends on, but having seen the way Xaphan moved, the confidence in his stride, she knew who would win against this undisciplined lot.

Sword flashing in one hand, a silver dagger in the other, her grumpy demon danced. Lunge. Swipe. Oops there went an arm. Stab. Turn. Ooh, that must have hurt.

Into the thin air, he disappeared, leaving his foes bewildered. Not for long. Only paces away he'd reappear, sometimes tapping on a shoulder to make it sporting. It didn't save the mob even when they whirled around quick. Against his sword and his skill, the folk of Swamptown, well, the belligerent bullies at any rate, died. The smart ones stood back and watched, while the damned souls, some of them foolish enough to get involved, got sliced and diced. Lucky for them, they couldn't die, just wail as they begged people to pull them back together. But the demons, and those actually born in this place and brought to it while still alive, they fell, never to rise again.

As the number of combatants dwindled, the vendor behind her grew silent, and when he made his move, she quickly shot out a hand and grabbed him by his greasy tunic.

"And where do you think you're going?" she asked. "We're not done yet."

As usual for his kind, he didn't believe her and tugged at her grip. Yeah, so he was bigger and stronger physically. Funny how the application of her knife in a few spots got him to behave himself. Xaphan finished off his last assailant, to her wild cheer of, "Go, grumpy, go!"

Turning to her, a half smile tilted his lips and although

he shook his head, and muttered, "Psycho female," she could hear the affection in his tone. It warmed her. It confused her. She took it out on the demon she sat on with an elbow pressed to his neck.

"Who is the guy that gave you the collar?" she demanded.

A gurgle was her reply.

"Act stubborn, will you? I know ways of making you talk."

A shadow fell over her as Xaphan returned to her side. "Um, Katie. Maybe you should let him breath so he can answer."

Oops. She removed her arm from his throat. "Answer."

Heaving in big gulps of air, the demon vendor babbled. "I don't know him. Swear I don't. He came in and traded the collar for some food, a wagon and a swamp salamander to pull it."

"Where was he going?"

"I don't know."

"Do you know what I do to demons who lie to me?" She pressed her knife below his remaining eye.

"South. They went south. I heard something about the Hairy Den in the ninth circle but that's it."

Kneeling beside her, Xaphan flicked the demon in the forehead. "Who's they?"

"Just a pair of yellow demons and their ugly lizard on a leash."

"Was it pink?"

"Could have been. Hard to tell with the mud all over and the blanket they'd tied to its back."

Standing, Katie sheathed her knives. "Lovely. I chipped my nails going through the swamp for nothing."

"What are you talking about? We now have a lead."

The vendor didn't crawl away like a smart demon, instead, he stared up at her jean covered crotch. She stomped on his groin before she moved away. "Bah. That's not a lead. It's where I intended to go if our hunt here didn't pan out. Everything illegal goes through the Hairy Den at one point or other."

"Should I ask why it's called Hairy?"

"Why tell when I can show you?"

He backed away, and she laughed. "Not on me, silly. That's shaved bald, this week at any rate. I like to alternate. When I said show, I meant the bar, in person. Unless you'd like to check me first to see if I'm telling the truth?"

"Uh, no thanks."

"Let me know if you change your mind. Or if you want to rub it for luck." She winked and laughed as a ruddy color crept up his cheeks. Damn but she loved it when he did that.

Digging inside her shirt, she yanked out an amulet and held it in front of her.

"What's that for?"

"Quick ticket home. Lucifer had it made for me on my birthday. It comes in handy for work." And the nights she was too drunk to walk home.

She incanted a word and a dark hole appeared before them, a portable portal that would lead back to the inner ring of Hell. About to step through, she halted and shuddered as something slimy slid over her ankle.

Before she could kill the demon, who dared lick her, Xaphan lopped off his head.

Mouth open wide, she stared at him.

With a nonchalance she found hot, he shrugged. "He

offended me. And you're not the only one with anger issues."

Laughing like a loon – and enjoying Xaphan more and more – she stepped through the hole, her grumpy enigma at her back.

6

WITH A FEW HOURS TO kill before he met with Katie – because this time he didn't think it worth the bother to try and ditch her – Xaphan went to meet with Lucifer who lounged in his theater room watching his brother, God, play golf across the heavens. Now there was a place he'd never get to visit, his sins too numerous, but given the reports he'd received of boredom and the number of angels that intentionally fell from grace just so they could have some fun, he counted his blessings.

"My Lord? May I speak with you a moment?"

Holding up a hand, Lucifer motioned him to silence and Xaphan studied the screen where God wound up, swung and sent the ball flying off the edge of a fluffy cloud. "Ha. I never tire of watching that shot." Turning to him, his boss smiled and motioned for him to approach. "Come in. Come in. I was just studying my opponent. I've got spies taping my brother's practices. Jerk's got great putting skills. Decent chipping ones, but he sucks around water and nothingness hazards. I've got to remember to tell my minions to make sure our tournament next week has plenty of them. Even if they've got to TNT the holes and import the H2O by hand."

"Everyone in Hell is rooting for you, sir." Every century, Lucifer, God and deities from the other planes that no one knew much about, got together for the tournament, Golf Across The Planes. His Lord had yet to win, but so long as he beat his brother, he usually returned in a jovial mood. The few times he hadn't, well, the tantrum he threw was felt by more than just the denizens of Hell. It wasn't just Mother Earth who could cause earthquakes.

"Of course they're cheering, because I am fabulous. Now if only I could decide on a caddy. Ever since last year's debacle where mine fell into that unfortunate pit of alligators on the sixteenth, it's been hard to find someone reliable."

Everyone heard about that one, and millions saw it on HBN – Hell's Broadcasting network. Lucifer's club went flying after his stroke and hit the slack jawed caddy upside the head. He stumbled back, arms wind milling and everyone watching heard the long, long scream as the bag carrier plummeted followed by the crunching as he got eaten. And during it all, Lucifer watched with a satisfied smile. Some said the punishment was too harsh but most thought the caddy totally deserved it, giving their Lord a seven iron in the sharp bladed rough when he needed a five to chip out.

"No matter who caddies for you, sir, you will prevail on skill alone." Ass kissing. You didn't live to a ripe demonic age without indulging in it from time to time.

Lucifer beamed. "Enough about my greatness. What brings you? Have you found the dragon yet?"

"No, but we have a good lead which we'll be checking out in the morning. I'm here actually on a personal matter." A matter he'd hemmed and hawed over, unable to come to a clear headed decision. With no real close friends – anger issues aside, most found his grim countenance a party downer – he went to the one person he oddly enough trusted.

"Uh-oh, you want me to assign you a new partner. I had a feeling this would happen. I know Katie can seem a little flighty, but I assure you, she's one of the best I've got."

"I know, sir, and I'm not here to have her removed. She's got great skills as a tracker and fighter. My problem is I'm having a hard time staying true to my vow."

"What vow? Do you mean the one you made to that harpy, what's her name again?"

Xaphan winced at Lucifer's insult but knew better than to correct him. "Roxanne, sir."

"Ah yes. Roxanne. Because of her you vowed to be a boring, stick in the mud who whacks off instead of getting laid."

Explained in such a crude nutshell it sounded remarkably stupid, but he still defended his decision. "I was staying true to my love, sir."

"Argh." Lucifer gagged. "Don't speak that word out loud. I hate it. Do you know Gaia keeps asking me to say it? Claims I need to be able to vocalize my affection. You'd think me yelling, 'Yeah baby, that's it, take it deep!' would be enough to show her what I feel. But no. She wants the

L word. Women! But you aren't here to hear about my relationship woes, or see the video, which I might add is quite the work of art. You have a dilemma of your own. And judging by your soul, and your face, I'd say the vow you made in the haste of your youth is coming back to haunt you. Or as I like to call it, you're suffering an extreme case of blue balls."

Despite what people thought, the Lord of Hell was an astute man who always understood his subjects and always came straight to the point, even if he lacked eloquence.

"I want to stay true to Roxanne. I made a vow and I mean to keep it. I need to know how to fight this unnatural attraction."

"I assume this involves Katie."

Who else? "Yes. When I'm around her, I forget about Roxanne and my vow. I want nothing more than to..."

"Bend her over and fuck her. Tickle her tonsils. Decorate her in pearls. Yes, I get the picture. Good thing you came to me. I've got a simple solution to your problem. Avoid Katie."

Not see her? Xaphan immediately dismissed the idea on the grounds he just didn't like it. "Avoiding her is the coward's route and impossible, given our task."

"So I'll release you from the job. Reassign you to the mortal side."

Xaphan shook his head. "No. I took on the mission and I will see it to the end with my partner. It's the honorable thing to do."

"I really wish you wouldn't say that aloud. It goes against everything I believe in."

"I forgot myself. What I meant to say was I want to kill the fucking bastards who dared steal from the greatest Lord of all the planes."

Lucifer beamed. "That's more like it. As for your dilemma with Katie, I see only one possible solution. Fuck her."

Now there was an answer his cock agreed with wholeheartedly, which was the root of his problem. "But that's what I'm trying to avoid."

A huff of air burst from Lucifer, and his eyes began to burn. "Listen, son. Have you forgotten who I am? You want to stay true to your vow and be all holier than thou, then talk to my brother. Me, nothing would make me happier than for you to break your stupid promise, rip the clothes from the girl and sin with her until the imps come home. But you already knew I'd say that which is why you came to me isn't it?"

Xaphan didn't even bother trying to lie when his boss zoomed right in on the truth. Yes he knew Lucifer would encourage him to do what he craved. "Is it evil to want a bit of happiness?"

"I am delighted to say it's totally selfish. But it's also normal. You made a promise a long time ago when you were just a boy without fully understanding the ramifications. You based it on an infatuation that you thought was love. You wouldn't be the first. And you won't be the last. Men are often ruled by their dicks. I blame the lack of blood in our brains for that. Stupid design if you ask me. The overwhelming urge to stick our pricks in something soft is our most common downfall. However, you have a choice to not keep living a mistake you made centuries ago. Hell is an ugly place. The damned ash makes it so hard to keep it clean, but just because you live amidst filth, and violence and sin, doesn't mean you can't grab happiness. Or in this case a pair of sweet cheeks made for slapping." Lucifer hopped out of his seat to do a hip thrust dance around the theatre room.

"I don't know. It sounds so easy when you say it. But what about after? Won't I feel guilt, or self-loathing?"

"Probably both which means you'll be back to your daily self-flagellating state. That should make you happy."

"What if I'm not?" What if he wanted to do it again and again? Would he turn into some sex crazed demon? *No, because there's only one female who seems to provoke a reaction.*

Lucifer cuffed him upside the head. "Stop thinking so hard about it and just do it. Blow off some steam. Give your swimmers some exercise. Then see how you feel."

"Maybe she'll say no?" He said it questioningly, but a part of him knew, once they kissed again, short of an audience or life threatening attack, there would be no stopping.

"She might. Or she might ride you like a pony on a bouncy trail and remind you what pleasure is. Oh, but, be careful once you do the naughty deed. My favorite psycho has anger issues."

"I know. It's one of the things I like about her."

"I always knew you were a freak somewhere inside," Lucifer said with a smile and a slap on his back. "Now go get her, and fuck her so hard she walks bowlegged for a week."

Forget a week, given his pent up sexual energy, if he did let loose, she could end up in a wheelchair with numb legs for a month.

As he pictured the various ways he could take her, it only vaguely occurred to him that he already seemed determined to forget his vow. Nudging even that small reminder aside was easy with the image of a pair of mismatched eyes staring at him, smoldering with desire, her lips parted with passion and with lust consuming his mind.

OFF XAPHAN WENT, LOOKING DETERMINED TO BED A certain crazy girl and Lucifer wanted to dance in glee. But he didn't want to jinx the situation, so instead he went looking for a snack. He'd just finished creating a decadent concoction when Katie came bouncing into the kitchen, in time to steal his heated chocolate brownie covered in whipped cream.

"My favorite! Thanks boss." Sucking the decadence off a spoon in a way that made him more than happy to give her the whole cake, Lucifer prepared another piece and waited. Sure enough, she'd come to talk about something other than his fabulous nature and the progress of her mission.

"How important is Xaphan in the whole minion deal?" she asked licking her finger after she trailed it through the cream.

"He's an excellent soldier."

"So you'd miss him if he was gone?" she queried before sucking on a hunk of brownie with her eyes closed while wearing a blissful expression.

"Katie," he said adopting his paternal, warning tone. "You better not be planning on killing him."

"Not exactly, but I was thinking of fucking him, if he can forget about his damned wife for long enough to do the dirty deed."

"Wife? He told you he was married." Pride suffused Lucifer at the lie his staid minion told.

"Not exactly. More like he was taken by a woman."

"Oh she took him alright," Lucifer muttered. "If you're worried about a jealous girlfriend chasing you down, then don't."

"So he's not in a relationship?"

"Not in the sense you think," he replied cryptically. He did so prefer to let events unfold on their own, with a little nudge from him, so he could sit back and watch the drama.

"It explains then why he had no problem sticking his tongue down my throat."

Startled, Lucifer gaped at her. "He kissed you?"

"Oh yeah, and he would have done more if I'd let him."

"Son of a gun, he left that part out when we were talking." A chuckle left him. Dirty demon. It made a devil want to wipe a tear of pride.

"He talked to you?"

He waved her query away. "Yes, but I can't discuss it. Confidential, man to man shit, you know. Suffice it to say, you've left an impression." More like slammed through the armor his soldier built around his heart. Just as he'd hoped.

Katie perked up. "So he was talking about me. Awesome."

"We're getting off topic. You were talking about having sex. I totally approve." It was after all part of his master plan.

"I was, but if I do decide to let him hitch a ride on the Katie train, am I allowed to kill him after?"

"I'd prefer you didn't. I find him quite useful. Katie," he adopted a softer, fatherly tone. It usually made his daughter, Muriel laugh her ass off, but his damaged psycho was another matter. "Are all these questions your way of telling me you like him?"

Not looking up, Katie stirred her spoon in the chocolate mess. "I don't like men."

"Human men. Xaphan's half demon."

"Demons are pigs too."

"Now you're generalizing. Has Xaphan done something to make you think he's not trustworthy?"

She scowled. "No. Do you know he even holds doors open for me? It's sick. I'm sure he's hiding an evil side, though. I think all his niceness is part of his wicked plan to get in my pants while pretending he has no interest."

"Oh he's hot for you, sweetie. He just hates himself for it," Gaia announced as she glided into the kitchen wearing a diaphanous gown that would look better on his bedroom floor.

"Self-loathing?" Katie perked up. "That's hot. So he won't get all clingy if we do it? I'd have to kill him for sure if he did."

"Nope. I have a feeling your half demon will go running once he does the deed with you. He's a dirty pig, just like all the rest." Gaia arched a brow at Lucifer over Katie's head and crowned her satisfied expression with a smirk.

"Would you stay out of it?" Lucifer hissed to his on and off again girlfriend.

Brilliant green eyes clashed with his. "No. You are not the only one who can dispense advice."

"I rule this domain." He thumped his fist for emphasis on the granite countertop.

"And?"

"And that means stay out of my employee business," Lucifer sputtered as she defied him.

"Just like you stayed out of my garden way back when?"

He groaned. "Are we back to that? Geez woman, that was like a million years ago. I was young, and bored. Look at the fun that came out of that whole apple incident. I'm the reason sex got invented."

"Ha. You wish. I'm the one who introduced horniness to all the animals in the world. You just got lucky when it caught you in the backlash."

"You mean you got lucky?" He leered at Gaia and made a grab for her. With a giggle, she darted away and he chased her around the kitchen island a few times before he caught her in his arms. Catching the tail end of Katie discreetly leaving, he nuzzled his girlfriend's neck. Mother Earth drove him nuts, but dammit, of all the women he'd ever had sex with – and those counted in the thousands – she was the only one who kept him coming back for more and more. But it wasn't love. Nope. Not for him. He just liked that thing she did with her tongue. And maybe her laugh.

Okay dammit. There were lots of things about her he liked, but he wasn't going to hand her his heart on a platter. Although, they were in a kitchen and he was still hungry...In moments her gown fluttered to the floor and she sat on a plate, legs spread, a feast for his taking.

Nothing like fresh pie. Green apple filling, sweet and tart, just the way he liked it.

As she yanked on his hair, his tongue busy, he managed to forget for a moment his master plan to rebuild his army. And when she later returned the favor on her knees, damn, he even forgot his name.

7

By the next morning, Xaphan wasn't any closer to a decision. When he'd left Lucifer, things seemed so clear. Find Katie. Fuck her until his balls were dry. Then go back to his lonely state, flagellating himself for betraying Roxanne.

Or...he could do something completely nuts, say, like forget his vow entirely and see where things with Katie went. Oh, but the idea intrigued him. Imagine, not waking to loneliness or a soul sucking darkness. To sleep with someone, for the first time since he'd never dared in his last hidden relationship. How would it feel to smile and share, openly, what Hell had to offer? Talk about temptation for a lonely soldier. *Why can't I be happy?* Hadn't he suffered enough?

He'd almost convinced himself he deserved a chance to live again, but then he'd mistakenly let himself glance at his shrine. He could have sworn Roxanne's eyes in the portrait stared upon him with disappointment. They accused him of being faithless. And no good.

It made him feel like the lowest creature in Hell.

But he didn't apologize. Couldn't squeeze the words past his lips. Wouldn't tell a lie – which surely pissed his Lord off. Despite the vow he'd made, the shame and guilt that he already battled, he couldn't help wanting Katie.

Cowardice, though, kept him from doing anything about it. He didn't stalk over to her apartment and sweep her off her feet. He didn't plan a seduction or a battle to get her into his bed. A part of him hoped she'd take the decision from him. Seduce him like she almost did in the swamp. Make it easy because, dammit it all, having never actually courted a woman, now that he'd found one who made him want to forget his vow, he didn't know what to do. Other than mope that was, and hurry to meet her, leaving early with a spring in his step and a determined look in his eyes that had the damned souls on the streets diving for cover.

Meeting with Katie by the portal to the ninth circle – damn she looked good, so sexy in a mini skirt that barely covered her mound, a halter top with no bra that delineated her nipples and her hair swept into a high pony tail – he throbbed with arousal as soon as he laid eyes on her. Forget his vow, their mission, everything. He just wanted to press her up against the nearest wall, suck on her full lower lips and sink into her heat.

"Hi, grumpy," she said with a wave and a smile. "Are you ready?"

Damn straight he was. Oh wait, she meant to go on their mission. "Yeah. But where's your weapons. We aren't exactly going on a picnic in the nice part of town."

A brilliant smile flashed his way. "Don't you worry about me, baby. I've got all the bases covered. Besides, with that *big* and *mighty sword* of yours, what else does a girl need?" She winked.

Somehow he didn't think she meant the sword sheathed down his spine. His chest swelled along with his cock.

"Nice coat," she remarked as they approached the portal. "But what happened to the other one? The one I borrowed?"

The reminder that he wore his battle scarred leather duster took care of some of his lust. "Somehow, my favorite coat got decorated with pink crystals. But you wouldn't know anything about that, would you?"

A snicker escaped her. "Who me? Okay. I'm guilty of dazzling your coat, but in my defense, I'm really hoping you'll give it to me."

For some reason he immediately thought of her naked wearing only the coat. "Come by my place after we're done today, and you can have it." And he didn't just mean the jacket she'd ruined. He also had something else to give her.

The squeal she uttered didn't entirely deafen him, but the enthusiastic hug and the warm kiss she pressed on his lips did leave him speechless. With a flounce and a giggle, she then disappeared into the portal. Sighing, for more reasons than he could count, Xaphan followed.

For those who weren't familiar with Hell, portals existed in various set locations in each of the nine circles. They were a quick way of getting around. Although if a being wanted to go via the more scenic route on the Styx with Charon as their guide, they could, there just wasn't any guarantee they'd make it. The denizens of Hell's longest river ever hungered for fresh meat.

Emerging from the transference point, the moment of teleportation a cold chill that sucked at the bones, he found Katie already sauntering up the dusty road. He split his attention between the shadows garnishing the alcoves in this forsaken place and the wiggle she put into her step.

"The Hairy Den is just up ahead," she announced as if the sign sporting a woman's mound covered in a bush thick enough to hide critters weren't enough. The ninth circle wasn't known for its class.

Catching up to her, he was just a pace behind her when she entered the noisy place. Early morning here didn't mean squat. Debauchery and drinking was a twenty four hour affair in Hell.

Stepping into the smoky room, Xaphan immediately went on alert scanning the faces and dismissing most as harmless. Dissolute, grey, and too drunk or high to care, the patrons barely spared him a moment's notice. Not so his psycho. Eyes tracked Katie's sashay into the bar, and more than a few orbs glinted with lust. It made him wish he'd brought a cloak to cover her with. But then again, he could always just blind the whole lot – a solution which would still allow him to enjoy her outfit.

Jealousy, what a novel emotion, one he rather enjoyed as it fed his hunger for violence. Never a bad thing.

Hopping onto a stool, which hiked Katie's micro mini even higher, she leaned forward and said, "A pina colada if you please, extra coconut, super frothy with a cherry on top."

Seriously? "Katie, what are you doing?" he whispered loudly as he came alongside her.

"Ordering a drink of course. What's it look like I'm doing?"

"But it's not even noon. And we have a job to do."

"It's noon somewhere in the world, isn't it boys?" she asked with a wide smile as she spun on her stool to face the crowd.

A cheer met her words along with a chorus of 'Aye' and 'Yes.'

"See?" she said peering at him with mismatched eyes that twinkled with mirth. "Stop being such a stick in the mud. Relax. Why don't you prop that sweet ass of yours on a stool, loosen the coat and order yourself something with a kick?"

"I don't drink." The last time he got drunk, he promised his Roxanne he'd save her from a marriage to an old man. He woke up the next morning, his soul, a possession of the devil, the old man in question dead, and his ass sprawled on the cold floor of the dungeon. Talk about a quick cure for alcoholism.

"Don't drink? But that's even more insane that I am! Pull up a stool, grumpy, because there's no time like the present to start." Clapping her hands, she bounced in her seat and a sigh went through the room. "Barkeep, bring my serious friend here a shot of your strongest brew."

Moments later, a bowl with a creamy white liquid topped with a bright red cherry and a sad looking umbrella appeared along with a questionably clean glass filled to the brim with an amber hued, smoking liquid.

"Katie, I don't think this is a good idea." And not just because of the lipstick clinging still to the side of the glass, or the fact the brew seemed to be eating away the inside of the glass.

She snorted. "You don't think anything is a good idea."

"Alcohol leads to impairment, probably not the wisest course of action given our location."

Laughter spilled from her. "Are you actually afraid a teensy tiny drink will hurt you? Chicken." She clucked a few times, her poor poultry imitation abetted by the crowd that snickered and jeered.

Straightening his spine, he glared at her. "I fear nothing."

"Then prove it."

Dammit. A challenge. Manhood called into question, did he have a choice? No. And she knew it too, the brat.

A smile of triumph tilted the corners of her lips. "Cheers!" Lifting her bowl, she sipped, then gulped. She drained the whole damned pina colada, finishing it with a satisfied sigh. Plucking the cherry from the empty container, she arched a brow and smirked in his direction.

"Your turn."

Xaphan eyed the glass dubiously. Poison. Battery acid. All would probably taste better than what fermented in the cup before him. However, goaded on by the derisive comments of the folk behind him, and the gaze of a psycho who dared him to do it, he picked it up, and before he could think about it, drank it.

"Holy. Fucking. Hell!"

SMOKE DIDN'T COME BURSTING FROM HIS MOUTH, BUT ONLY barely. Katie bit her lip as her grumpy demon, red faced and eyes wide, tossed back a shot of Hell's Lava. Naughty of her to dare him, but really, someone needed to help him loosen up. Not having a mountain giant to stomp on his back, alcohol was the next best thing. And so what if she had another ulterior motive to getting him drunk such as getting the crowd to spill its secrets, something that wouldn't happen if they thought Xaphan was an uptight tool.

"Another," she ordered.

"I shouldn't."

This time, she didn't need to goad him, the patrons did it for her.

"Lucifer's man is a pussy."

"Hey princess, I think you forgot your tiara at home."

"What's a pretty girl like her doing with a pansy fucker like him?"

Five drinks later, her demon slumped over the bar, eyes closed, and the stage was set. Hopping onto the bar, pretending to weave a little, Katie held up her newest drink – she had a remarkable head for alcohol which won her many a wager in the bars – and cocked a hip, knowing where all eyes would focus. It was, after all, why she'd worn her pinkest panties.

"Since my friend is out for the count. I need a new partner, if you know what I mean." She winked, then laughed as hands shot up all over the place and waved madly. "Me! Me! Pick me!"

"Goodness, look at all the eager demons. Oh and even a few damned souls. But how's a girl to choose." She pretended to tap her chin in thought and bopped her hips from side to side, holding in a giggle as heads went bobbing back and forth following the motion. "Ooh, I know. How about whoever brings me the coolest present wins?"

A flurry of movement took over the room as hands

went rummaging in pockets, bags, and fights broke out as thefts occurred. Useless paper money fluttered. Gold coins bounced. A set of teeth narrowly missed her feet.

"Boys. Boys!" she shouted. "I don't see anything I like. I want something special. Something rare."

"Like what?" a noxious green demon asked.

"Oh, I don't know. But it should be unique. Oh and pink. I do so love pink."

Crude comments flew about the pink the crowd loved, and they weren't talking about her panties.

Males. So predictable. "Um, boys, we weren't talking about my pink prize. Who's going to give me the biggest pink present?" And finally, short of telling them outright, she heard the words she wanted to hear.

"How's about a pink dragon?"

Pointing to the horned demon who'd shouted, she waved him over. Batting her lashes, she buttered him up. "Did you say a dragon? I've always wanted one of those. But are you sure it's pink? I thought they only came in green and black."

"Seen it myself," he boasted. "Not even two days ago."

"So you don't actually have it?"

"No. But I knows one of the fellows that does. Stinky Pete and I goes way back."

"Stinky Pete," she mused. "Why does that name sound familiar?"

"'Cause he's the biggest demon smuggler 'tween here and the mortal side, that's why."

She snapped her fingers. "Of course. Pete's Emporium of Junk and Stuff. Thanks." Hopping down from the bar, she evaded the demon's grasping claws. She tapped

Xaphan on the shoulder. He raised his head and opened one bleary eye.

"Wh-a-a-t?" He slurred the word as he bathed her face in breath that could have caused an explosion if lit.

"Time to go, grumpy."

He slid off the stool, slumped, then caught himself, blinking at the room at large.

"What happened?"

"You got drunk and danced naked on the bar."

"No way!" He looked down at himself and frowned. "You're joking."

"Hoping. I don't suppose now that I've mentioned it you'd be inclined to give me a show?"

Xaphan shook his head and glared at someone behind her. "Why is that demon trying to hug you?"

The demon in question was actually trying to cop a feel, but only her sly jiggles from side to side kept him from getting a grip. "Oh him? He thinks we're going to have sex." She leaned up and hoping Gaia hadn't misled her about Xaphan's interest, whispered. "I told him that the only demon I wanted was you, but he won't listen. He then touched me, even though I said no."

"He what?" Xaphan roared and his spine straightened as fury – and a bit of alcohol induced rage – gripped him. Shoving her aside, so he could stand in front of her, he eyed the squat demon up and down.

The idiot actually tried to push Xaphan aside.

"Get out of the way. I wants to collect my prize."

"She's mine," Xaphan snapped. "Keep your claws to yourself or else."

"Else what?"

"I am not arguing with a brainless fuck like you."

Quicker than she could blink, her grumpy demon drew his sword and lopped her informants head off.

Ooh. She said it in her head, but the patrons in the bar chorused it aloud. She clapped her hands. "Again."

Shooting her a look over his shoulder, Xaphan saw her grin, and to her surprise an answering smile, a wicked one, spread across his face. He winked. "My pleasure."

Sword swinging, Xaphan, looking utterly dangerous and delicious, waded into the now rampaging patrons. Most were too drunk to put up much of a fight, but there were still enough with their wits about them to make for some great action, and she watched avidly, in between kills of her own.

It seemed they'd bought her girly act a little too well. Some thought to claim her while her partner was otherwise occupied. Palming the daggers she'd hidden in the waist band of her skirt, she quickly disabused them of the notion.

Soon a pool of blood surrounded Katie and her partner, a deadly circle littered with bodies, limbs and groaning victims. Chest heaving, her grumpy demon turned to face her. Eyes glittering, still looking fierce, he took two long strides and without even sheathing his bloody sword, scooped her up in his spare arm, and kissed her.

WHILE HE DIDN'T REMEMBER MUCH AFTER THE THIRD drink, as soon as Katie whispered that another dared to touch her, he sobered quick, or at least enough to shake off the stupor and take care of all the eyes daring to leer at her. As he taught them the dangers of looking upon his psycho, he caught glimpses of her as she, with an expression of glee, dispatched the few who skirted him heading for her. Knives moving in a blur, she sliced and slashed, severing tendons and dumping her assailants in to boneless heaps.

Bloody. Violent. So many words to describe the ease with which she killed. The one that summed it up best of all though? Hot. So fucking hot.

Which was why when the room cleared of beings to kill and maim, he didn't stop but headed straight for the source of the burning inside him. Lips parted, eyes shining bright, Katie met his kiss with a passion he'd dreamt of for the past few days. Lifting her with his one free arm, he hugged her to his chest, not flinching at all when she brought her hands, still holding her knives, around his neck to embrace him tightly.

Who cared if she held a sharp weapon inches from his jugular when her tongue swept into his mouth, the flavor of her more intoxicating than any liquor?

"Hey. Who's going to pay for this fucking mess?" growled a voice.

Interrupted, and not happy about it, Xaphan lifted his head and glared at the burly barkeep who'd hidden behind his counter during the brawl. "Can't you see I'm busy?"

"Yeah, I can, and just so you know, it's a gold doubloon per hour for a private room, unless you don't mind me videotaping and selling the result on the Hellwide net."

One headless bartender later, Xaphan strode from the bar, dragging Katie by the hand.

"Where are we going?" she asked.

"Find. Bed. Now." Sentences were beyond him with

the adrenaline of battle wearing off and the dizzying effect of the alcohol, and her lingering kiss, rendering him incoherent.

"My poor, horny demon." She giggled. "Come with me and I'll make it all better."

Just what he wanted.

Fingers laced in his, she led the way, and a chilling portal later, which helped clear his mind, but did nothing for his aching cock, they were back in the inner circle. Skipping and tugging, she led him through a warren of side streets, and when he would lag, as his mind tried to question his actions, she'd whirl and kiss him until he stumbled along again, an eager slave to her will – a slave to his desire.

Entering a building, they climbed stairs, each landing burning more and more of his drunken haze. *If I go up there we're going to have sex. I will break my vow.*

He understood that, and fuck it all, he didn't care. A wildness consumed him, and he could no longer find the will to care about anything other than finally quenching the insatiable hunger inside. A hunger for Katie and Katie alone.

No longer battling himself, he took note of his surroundings, but the stairway with its wrought iron railing and stone steps couldn't hold his interest. The glimpses he kept catching of Katie's panties as she bounced up the steps, though, now that kept his interest piqued. Sheathing his sword finally, the metal one, not the flesh one – but that was coming real soon – he caught up to her and pulled his hand free.

When she whirled to protest, he picked her up and took the stairs two at a time.

The giggle as she clutched at him rang like music to his ears. "You'll wear yourself out. It's still two more flights."

"It's you that needs to worry about stamina," he growled. "It's been more than three hundred years since I've had a woman."

"Thanks for the warning," she whispered in his ear. "That means I better take care of you first so you've got time to recover for the main event."

Not sure what she meant, but more eager than ever to find out, Xaphan sprinted the last few steps and booted open the door to the hallway.

"Number?" he growled.

"Last one on the end."

Arriving at the door, decorated in a wreath of dead bunnies, real ones, he let her slide down the length of his body, and then placed his hands on her waist as she unlocked the door. She no sooner stepped in than he crowded in behind her, slamming the door shut only a second before he pressed her up against a wall, finally allowing himself to kiss her again. He'd only held off this long for the promise of privacy. No eyes but his were allowed to see Katie in all her naked glory.

Speaking of which... Seams were such fragile things and didn't last long with a pair of hands determined to rend them apart. In moments, her clothes lay in tatters on the floor and he swallowed hard at the beauty of her. Wide hipped, indented waist, round belly with a twinkling jewel in the middle, and heavy breasted, every inch of her was womanly, and *mine*.

Possessive or not, he intended to lick, caress and discover every inch of her. To imprint himself upon her creamy skin. To mark her with his cream. To...

Holy. Fuck.

Before he'd finished drinking his fill of her, she'd unbuckled his pants and pulled him free. Dropping to her knees, she never lost her grip on him, sliding her tight grip back and forth on his dick. Bracing a hand on the wall, he couldn't help thrusting into her caress.

"What are you doing?" he grunted.

"Me?" She peered up at him, big eyes rounded in innocence. "Having lunch, of course." Then she sucked him into her mouth and Xaphan just about exploded.

Teeth gritted, he tried to hold back as she suctioned his length. Stopping every so often, she would lick his cock, swirling her tongue around his swollen cap before taking him deep again. He'd never experienced anything like it. Never imagined how good it could feel. And it had been so long since another touched him. With a bellow that shook the plaster, he shot his cream. The greedy minx took it, her mouth never stopping its decadent torture.

"Enough," he groaned finally, his sensitized skin too much to handle.

"Mmm. If you insist." But that didn't stop her from teasing him. She moaned her pleasure into his flesh as she kissed her way back up his body, nipping his skin as she helped him shuck his clothes. A frenzied moment later, he stood just as naked as her.

He hugged her close, the skin to skin touch, electric and satisfying on a level he couldn't explain. But the hunger she'd just eased wasn't so easily appeased. With her soft skin brushing against his, her lips sucking at the flesh of his neck and her hands roaming his back, his desire roared back with a vengeance.

Weaving a hand into her hair, he tugged until her face lifted and she gazed upon him.

"Kiss me," he ordered.

She lifted herself on tiptoe and brushed her mouth over his. He sucked in a breath at the sensual slowness of it. But he'd waited far too long for a languorous exploration.

With a groan of need, he crushed his mouth to hers, taking her hungrily. She didn't mind his passion. Climbing him, she wrapped her legs around his waist, her moist core pressing wetly against his stomach. The knowledge he excited her as much as she did him almost brought him to his knees. He retained enough wits and strength to instead stumble further into her apartment, an open-plan loft that made it easy for him to weave his way to the bed.

Tossing her on the mattress, she giggled and bounced, her legs splaying apart, revealing her pink perfection. Grabbing her ankles, he yanked until her bottom came even with the edge of the bed. He spread her wide so he could admire. Despite its recent work out, his cock stirred to life as, unashamed, she held herself open for him, her pussy shaved liked mentioned, glistening damply with the evidence of her arousal. Utter, fucking perfection. *For me. And only me.*

"Don't just stare." She wiggled her hips. "Touching is expected, and wanted."

Oh, he'd touch her alright. Dropping to his knees, still holding her spread for his delight, he rubbed the edge of his jaw against the soft skin of her inner thigh. She gasped, and a shiver went through her body. He skipped the core of her to rub against the other leg, delighting in the sensation and the scent of her, her arousal, a drugging perfume like no other.

"Touch me, Xaphan." Her husky command made his cock twitch.

Pushing her legs up, he brought himself close enough to her sex to blow on it. Her hips arched, and a pleased chuckle slipped from him. Again, he let his hot breath caress her and her low moan rolled over him.

"Dammit. Stop teasing me."

Teasing her? What about him? His cock strained and ached, wanting to plunge into her velvety sheath. He wanted nothing more than to fuck her. But, he'd not forgotten what she'd done for him, and he meant to return the favor.

One lick, a sweet taste of her nectar, and he didn't care what his dick wanted. Oh, how he suddenly hungered. Needed. Wanted. He feasted on the core of her, nibbling at her tender flesh, lapping at her sex and flicking her nub. Under his ministration, she went wild. Her hips bucked. She panted. Just about ripped out his hair.

He fucking loved it. Spearing his tongue into her, he reveled in the tight feel of her as she clamped down, but he couldn't get deep enough. He let go of an ankle so he could thrust two fingers into her moist sex while he tongued her clit.

A wild scream ripped from her throat as she came, her muscles clenching his digits so tight. Holy fuck. He kept lapping at her while pumping his fingers into her quivering sheath.

It felt so fucking good. But wait, if it felt that great on his fingers, how much better would it be on his cock? As soon as the thought hit him, he had to know.

Positioning himself over her, he stared down into her flushed face and the mismatched eyes that gazed up at him with smoldering passion.

She took his breath away. She made his heart stutter. She made him *feel*.

Despite his desperate need, he sank into her slowly, enjoying every decadent inch of heat and wetness enveloping him. Only once he was fully sheathed did he realize he gritted his teeth. Buried deep inside her, her flesh still shuddering around him from her recent orgasm, it was almost too much to take. He wouldn't be able to hold for long from climaxing. *But by all the imps in Hell, I am not coming alone.*

XAPHAN TOOK HER WITH SUCH TORTUROUS, YET pleasurable, slowness, his gaze locked onto hers. What did he see when he looked at her? The blonde psycho she showed to the world, or did he actually see past that? The gentle way he treated her seemed to say *yes*. However, gentleness wasn't something she was accustomed to. It felt nice. She didn't trust it. She wanted more. She…

Too much thinking. She closed her eyes, unwilling to let herself succumb to anything but the wonder of the moment. Too long had she treated sex as a bodily need. To suddenly let emotions cloud it didn't suit her at all, even if he was the first to manage it. She wouldn't dwell on what it meant. What he meant to her. She would just let herself take what he offered – a long, slow fuck, driving her even further insane.

"Look at me," he growled.

She clamped her eyes tighter. He buried himself deep and swirled his hips, the tip of him rubbing against her special spot. She gasped.

"I said look at me," he ordered, and despite knowing she shouldn't, her lids flickered open.

Gazes locked, he continued to grind himself into her, touching her in a way that kept making her suck in air with a gasp. Clasping her legs, he pushed them toward her head and leaned over her, never losing sight of her eyes. It was so fucking intense. So intimate. So right.

Her second climax hit with agonizing slowness, her body tightening and squeezing, the pressure almost painful. As the tension in her peaked, his cock pulsed and she crashed over the edge, her flesh undulating with waves of pleasure that made her lose sight of everything even though her eyes remained open.

She heard him cry her name. Felt him spill deep inside her. And dammit, if she didn't know better, she'd have said the tiny part of her soul still belonging to her, touched his.

A moment later, maybe several, she came back to Hell to find herself cradled in his arms. Cuddling. What the fuck? Didn't he know males had lost body parts for daring to do less?

It occurred to her she should say something, or grab a knife and order him out. But with his hands stroking soothing circles on her skin, and his lips brushing her temples with a gentleness she'd never known, or allowed, she instead fell asleep. And for the first time in her life, she wasn't alone – or bathed in blood.

8

XAPHAN WOKE to find Katie straddling him, but not with lustful intent. Unless she knew some kinky moves to go with the knife she held at his throat.

"Morning?" He didn't move lest he startle her into action.

"Try goodbye."

That didn't sound promising. "Can I ask why? I thought we both enjoyed ourselves last night." Or was he so woefully out of practice, she'd rather kill him than risk him trying again?

"We did."

Phew. "But?"

"We had sex."

"Yes." Several times. Once in the shower when he carried her there after a nap. Then again after their exploratory cleansing. Oh and in the middle of the night because he couldn't resist touching her.

"Don't you understand? We had sex, which means I have to kill you."

"I see." He didn't, but he'd find out. Sure, he heard the rumors and the hints, but never actually expected her to attempt it. Not after what they shared. "If you're going to do it," he stated calmly, not looking away from her, or flinching. "Then please hurry, because I'm hungry."

Indecision swam in her eyes. She sucked on her lower lip as her hand trembled. "I don't want to kill you." She said it sadly.

"I'd also prefer you didn't."

"I have to."

"No, you don't. You could instead put the knife down." The point pressed deeper. "Or not," he hastened to add. "Keep the knife if you like, but it will make it harder for you to hold onto me."

"You want to have sex?"

He shrugged. "I was thinking more of a snuggle before breakfast."

"I don't snuggle. And I don't do repeats."

"You did last night." Okay, that came out a little boastful. How could he resist when he heard her say she never usually went back for seconds? *And I got a quadruple helping. Who's the greatest demon lover? Me!*

"Last night was an anomaly. An aberration. It won't and can't happen again. I'm the Black Widow. You must have heard of me."

Katie was the Black Widow? Yeah, he'd heard of her. All demons had, but no one knew who she was or what she looked like? Killing her victims before they could boast tended to do that. "Actually, I have heard of you. And?"

"What do you mean, *and*? Just like the spider, I kill those I bed."

He smirked. "So what if you killed your past lovers? It just leaves me more spare time."

"Now I'm confused. How does my reputation leave you more spare time?"

"If they're already dead, then it will save me the bother of hunting them down."

The pressure on the knife at his neck eased as she leaned back. Her brow creased. "Hunt them down for what?"

"You have anger issues. I have jealousy ones." The mere thought of someone else even so much as breathing near her bothered him.

His reply took her aback. "You would kill someone for fucking me?"

"Torture perhaps too. And that goes for touching. Kissing. Propositioning. Oh, and possibly staring too long."

"You're insane," she breathed.

"I prefer the term possessive."

"No man owns me."

"I don't want to own you."

"Then what do you want?"

Hmm, the words 'I want you forever' came to mind but that was too quick to announce even for him, especially with her intimacy issues, oh and the knife in the bed with them. But he did settle for another truth. "I want you under me, clawing my back again."

At his claim, her nipples pearled, and she licked her lips. "I don't do repeats."

"Always a first time."

For a moment he thought he had her. The hand with the knife dropped to her side, she squirmed on him, then she shook her head and an almost sad expression crossed her face. "I wish I didn't have to kill you."

"Then don't."

"But I have a reputation to uphold. If I let you live, they'll think I'm weak. They'll try to hurt me. Use me."

"Then I will kill them." And he would. Tear them limb from limb if they dared to even think of going near her.

"I don't understand you. You don't even like me."

"I don't like a lot of people. You, however, have grown on me."

"Like a fungus?"

He winced. "Not exactly how I'd explain it, but I guess it works."

"So where do we go from here?"

"Well, if you don't kill me, I thought we'd get some breakfast."

"Donuts?"

"If you like, or bacon with eggs."

The knife pressed again. "I hate eggs."

"Then we'll skip eating them and save them for throwing at people from the window."

She grinned. "You wouldn't?"

If she smiled like that at him? He'd do anything. Even say stupid things apparently. "Listen, why don't we take things slow? Eat, go find ourselves a dragon, and see where things go from there." Although he could already see them ending up in his bed. Maybe his counter. Definitely over his couch.

Or according to the lips that suddenly clung to his, maybe right here, right now. If she wanted to go again, he wouldn't say no.

His hands clasped her full buttocks, loving the round

softness of them. A part of him wondered, as he palpated her flesh, if the bite he'd given her the previous night still marred her creamy skin. He hoped so. He liked the idea of her wearing his brand almost as much as he loved seeing her wearing his cock.

A groan slipped past his lips when she lifted herself from his body, then slammed back down, sheathing his eager dick. Fuck, even after all the times they'd made love, he couldn't get over how he felt when buried to the hilt inside her. How she roused emotions he'd thought lost forever plus some he'd never known. Those wishy-washy musings got lost in his fascination with her jiggling breasts.

Creamy in color, heavy and natural, topped with a hard berry, they made him hungry. He slid his hands up her back so he could pull her down for a taste. The puckered tip of one slid into his open mouth and he sucked hard, pulling a cry from her. Apart from the sound, he could tell her enjoyment from the way her channel tightened around his buried shaft. He grazed her nipples with his teeth, one after the other, teasing them, blowing on them, before sucking them into his mouth again, one by one.

While he played with her delectable tits, she rode him, her bottom lifting and dropping on his cock, each slam of her flesh against his driving his passion higher and higher. She took away his berries and gave him her lips, her body moving into a rhythmic, gyration on his cock. He clasped her about the waist, pushing her down hard on his dick. Forcing her to take him as deep as she could. She mewled her pleasure against his lips, her breathing frantic.

This time, when he said, "Look at me," she didn't fight

EVE LANGLAIS

it. She opened her glorious mismatched eyes, the intimacy and passion in them arousing him as surely as her grinding body. He could tell the moment she came, and not because of her convulsing muscles, but because her eyes fluttered, her body arched into a taut bow, and something warm, something not of the physical plane, but esoteric, touched him. Marked him. Bound them together more surely than any vow, ring or ceremony.

Whether she'd admit it or not, she belonged to him. Not that he said anything stupid like that aloud as they recovered, sweaty and panting on her sheets. But the moment needed something to temper the intensity.

Toying with his mortality, he slapped her on the ass and said, "Woman, make me some breakfast."

She laughed so hard she fell out of bed. And lucky him, he got to kiss her bruised posterior before he fucked her, again.

After a leisurely breakfast of donuts, bacon and coffee in a nearby diner – making food poisoning less likely – where she flirted outrageously and he glared at anything that dared look her way, they separated so he could go grab a shower and change of clothing. They planned to meet in two hours by the portal for the mortal side. The separation already chafed him.

Sailing into his apartment, he only hesitated a moment when he caught sight of his altar. The accusation in the portrait's eyes didn't even give him a twinge of guilt. He felt nothing, actually, but relief.

I'm free!

Hot damn. And he owed it all to a psycho named Katie.

Thinking of whom, he'd have to get rid of the picture and shrine before she saw it. After his shower, on his way to meet Katie, he'd dump it down the garbage chute, which went straight into the incinerator. The idea of toasting this link to his past to a crisp didn't hurt as expected. Lucifer was right. Xaphan had a right to happiness. He'd done his time in the trench of misery. Given enough to a love he no longer remembered.

It was time to live again. Maybe even to love? Just thinking of Katie – *my woman* – spurred him to action. The longer he dallied, the longer until he was by her side. Perhaps he'd hurry and meet her at her place. Or not. A male should play it cool.

Fuck that. Where she was concerned, he burned hot, and given how leery she seemed of relationships, he'd have to prove to her he wasn't going anywhere, even if she did threaten to kill him. Or tried. But he sure as well wanted to know who'd hurt her enough to make her feel that a moment of intimacy like they shared, required a death sentence.

Maybe I'll ask the boss later, after we drop off the dragon. Or I could wait until she trusts me enough to tell me herself. He could also torture it out of her.

He discovered, if he applied his tongue a certain way, Katie would do just about anything – scream his name, beg him to fuck her, even promise she'd learn how to cook – if he'd just let her come. Now there was a memory to cherish.

Fuck, did he miss her sappy as it made him. He needed to hurry so he could return to her side, where he belonged.

READY EARLIER THAN EXPECTED, WAY EARLIER BECAUSE SHE rushed on purpose, Katie got a hold of Xaphan's address and went to find him. She still wasn't sure what to do about the serious demon. Although, she could admit she liked the new Xaphan, the intriguing demon who seemed to emerge only for her. That demon had a sense of humor and killing streak almost as awesome as hers. Together they formed an unstoppable pair.

Together, as in a couple?

The very concept stopped her in her tracks. Since when did she feel comfortable pairing herself, even if mentally, with another person? Was it possible she'd finally healed enough from her past to contemplate letting someone get close to her again? To let Xaphan live, even though he'd seen her at her most vulnerable?

Is he my prince?

It still shocked her that she fell asleep, sheltered in his arms. Usually after sex, she killed the guy. A dead man couldn't boast he banged the devil's killer. And he couldn't get all clingy, either.

She had issues with males who tried to get close to her. While it took decades with her shrink, she'd finally gotten to the point where if things didn't pass third base, and she was in a good mood, she simply maimed instead of killed. Progress, right?

But Xaphan – not only did he bring her to ecstasy numerous times, he walked out the door, all his body parts intact. And this despite the fact he'd snuggled her. Cuddled her close as if he liked her, and more shocking, she enjoyed it. Actually, she looked forward to seeing him again, and not just because he was a naughty demon in bed. He woke feelings in her she thought long dead. Made her want the affection his gaze promised, the protection of his arms. *It would be nice to not be alone and the only one looking out for me.* It would be even nicer to keep the warm, fuzzy feeling he incited, and maybe even see where things with him could go – other than naked in bed. *Am I ready for something a little more permanent?*

Crazier even than her usual thoughts. And so confusing. Walking along Hell's streets, lost in her thoughts, thinking of Xaphan and wondering what to do, she lashed out at the poor demon who dared say "Hey hot stuff, wanna fuck?' He suffered for his comment by losing his tongue. The violence didn't clear the turmoil in her mind but it did make her giggle. It also reminded her of who she was and what she could do. If things got too complicated with Xaphan or too hard for her to handle, her knife could always make things better.

Arriving at Xaphan's building, a mirrored glass monstrosity stretching high in the sky, she amused herself, pushing all the buttons in the elevator, then took the stairs. The locked door to his condo took her only a moment to pick. Knocking was for the polite, and boundaries didn't exist in Katie's world. Besides, she wanted to surprise Xaphan.

Of course, once inside, she found herself torn. The audible evidence of a running shower, which meant a naked, probably horny, demon, or the white mantle covered in a fine cloth with a small, framed painting, sitting atop.

Who held such a place of prominence?

On silent feet, she crossed to the image and lifted it. She instantly hated the woman depicted. With her perfectly upswept hair, Mona Lisa fucking smile and matching eyes, Katie knew she'd found the woman Xaphan loved. If it were a contest of looks, she'd lose. No way could she match the perfection she saw. Not with her wild blonde hair and mismatched eyes.

Didn't Xaphan say it had been three hundred years though since he'd touched a woman?

She was sure he had, which meant the paragon in the image might have died. Peeking around his place, she noted the austere setting. No color. Not a single plant or knickknack. Nothing in the place screamed a woman lived there. Apart from the shrine, she would have said Xaphan was single.

But his heart was taken. She held the evidence in her hands.

"What are you doing here?" Cold and brusque, his voice startled her into dropping the frame. It hit the floor with a crack, the glass pane covering it shattering.

Wincing, she peeked up at him. The horror in his eyes would have appeared comical if she weren't so pissed at his initial reaction to her snooping. "Oops?" Then to make sure her sarcasm was clear, she ground the image into the floor and shards of glass. It helped to keep her attention away from the fact Xaphan stood across the room in nothing but a towel. And damn, despite the fact he cared for another, he looked so fucking tasty with his bulging muscles slick from the water, begging for a lick.

"It's not what you think."

"Really? Are you telling me this isn't a shrine to the woman you love?"

"Yes, but –"

"Don't make excuses. I'm not fucking blind. Who is

she?" Planting her hands on her hips, Katie let her angry gaze meet his troubled one.

"If you'd let me explain –"

"I said who is she?"

"Roxanne. The woman I loved when I led a human life." The words dragged from him slowly and stabbed at her heart.

Pain consumed her, not that she let it show. This was what happened when a girl thought she could trust a man. He turned around and broke her heart. Okay, not quite the same situations as her youth, but still, the pain was very real, and all his fault. "So where is the saint who needs a shrine?"

"Dead, I figure, given how long ago we both lived. In Heaven, I imagine."

Katie rolled her eyes. "Wow. I can't believe you said that with a straight face. You know the population of Heaven is like one to every billion down here. What makes you so sure this *woman* earned some wings?" Was his precious Roxanne truly that pure? If yes, then Katie, with her innumerable sins, would never compare.

Doubt creased his brow. "I don't know where she is. I just always assumed she went to Heaven. I made a vow to never love another until we were reunited. Surely if she'd ended up in Hell, she would have found me."

"Re-e-a-a-l-l-ly?" Katie drew out the word. "Hello, oh gullible demon, since you believe that, would you be interested in buying some magic beans?"

"I'm not gullible."

"Says the man who's in love with a picture."

"I kept the painting as a reminder."

Katie's heart cracked a little further as he didn't deny

his love for the other woman. It made her angry. "Why did you need a picture? Was she that forgettable, because baby, now that we've fucked, I doubt you'll ever forget me."

"It always comes down to sex with you doesn't it," he retorted angrily. "Did it ever occur to you that what Roxanne and I had was more than fucking?"

"So you're telling me you didn't flip up her skirts and give it to her?"

The red cheeks answered her, but he still blustered ahead. "Of course we expressed our affection in a physical fashion. But there was more to our love than that."

"Really? Okay then what was her favorite color."

"I don't know but she wore a lot of blue."

Annoyed at his continued defense of this other woman, a dead woman no less, Katie fired questions at him. "Favorite food? Flower? Dreams she had? Names she planned for her first child? Dessert that made her close her eyes and groan?"

His mouth snapped shut.

"You don't know any of that do you, yet you claim to love her, this dead woman, who's probably been in Hell all this time and never bothered to look you up. You're an idiot."

"And you're psycho."

"Yeah, I am, but better crazy than stupid. And to think I let you live."

"Katie." He sighed her name and rubbed his face. "I don't want to fight with you. You were never supposed to see this."

"Why? Because I wasn't good enough to bring home to screw? Not as pretty as your Roxanne?" she spat, hating the tears in her eyes. "I knew I should have killed you."

"Would you stop and let me explain?"

"Explain what? That you fooled me into thinking I meant something? All along you just used me, used my body, while you thought of another. I hate you." She punctuated her words with a throw of her knives and while he dodged, she took off running.

Tears running down her cheeks, she bolted to the only person who ever offered her comfort. The only person she could trust. Lucifer.

Barreling through his antechamber, she ignored his secretary's hollered, "Stop!" and burst into his office.

"I want permission to kill him," she exclaimed before her eyes could fully grasp what was going on. Slapping a hand over her face, she shrieked. "My eyes. I'm blind. Help me! Argh!"

A snicker met her exclamation, from Gaia of course. Lucifer, whose tanned buttocks met her as she charged in, growled, "This isn't funny."

"Oh yes it is," Mother Earth replied still giggling. "It's why I like Katie. She's not in awe of you and tells it like it is."

Hearing the sound of fabric rustling and a zipper pulling, Katie peeked through her fingers. "Is it safe? Has the moon set?"

"Impertinent chit."

"Oh hush, you big bully." Gaia slapped Lucifer's arms.

"Me? This is my office, bloody hell. What's this plane of existence coming to if a man can't even pillage his girlfriend on the desk without getting interrupted? Whatever happened to knocking?"

"Ooh, I know the answer!" Katie waved her hand but didn't wait for permission to answer. Adopting her best, gruff voice, she said, "Knocking is for those with manners. And we all know I hate those."

Gaia cracked up, and Katie joined her while Lucifer glowered at them both.

"You are not funny at all," he muttered through gritted teeth.

"But dearest, she's right. You do say that all the time."

"Maybe, but it sounds grander when I do."

"If you say so, boss," Katie agreed. She and Mother Earth chortled a little more and Lucifer sighed.

"Okay, if we're done making fun of me, was there a reason you interrupted my midmorning tango?"

Immediately sobering, Katie remembered her reason for coming. "I want permission to kill him."

"Who? Did you find the miscreant who stole the dragon? You can kill him. Or torture him. Hell, you can even bring him back here for processing. I'm in need of a new chipping club. I accidentally snapped mine."

Sometimes her boss could act so dense. "No, no, and no. I want to kill the jerk you paired me with."

"Xaphan? What did the boy do? Did his sour puss finally get on your last nerve?"

"No. The stupid jerk made me like him."

"The cad!" Gaia exclaimed.

"I know," Katie moaned. "I can't stand it."

"Whoah. Rewind. You like him so you want to kill him. Shouldn't you instead be celebrating this victory? Your shrink's been waiting for this to happen for the last fifty some years."

"Xaphan is not my prince charming."

"Didn't you just say you liked him? Wasn't that what your doctor said you needed to heal?"

"Yes. But then he hurt me! He needs to die."

"How did he hurt you, sweetie? Come tell Mother Earth what the big bad demon did."

Lucifer snorted. "Isn't that just like a woman to assume *he* did something. Did it ever occur to you that maybe it's Katie's fault? She is crazy."

When dual glares were directed his way, Lucifer threw up his hands and stalked off, muttering something about going where he was wanted.

Gaia patted the seat across from her and Katie approached, sinking into the soft leather. "We're alone now, sweetie. Tell me what happened."

"We had sex."

"Naked?"

"Well duh."

"I'm impressed. He never strips down, not even to work out. I've got to ask, since no one's ever seen Xaphan out of his leather coats, what's his bod like?"

"Ridiculously hot. The guy is built like a god."

Gaia grinned. "I knew it. Go on. So you had fabulous sex, then what?"

"We cuddled." Even admitting it aloud made her cringe.

"You? And Xaphan?" Gaia goggled her. "Okay, I'll admit I wasn't expecting that. Good for you. You let someone get close. So what happened next?"

"We kind of had sex a few more times. And then in the morning, we shared some donuts and split up so he could go to his place to change and stuff."

"But I get the impression you still liked him at

this point?"

"Yes. Enough I decided to surprise him at his condo. Did you know the jerk has a shrine to some woman he loves? A fucking shrine!"

"Oh dear."

"'Oh dear' is right," Katie snarled. "I broke his picture. Accidentally, but I'm not sorry I did."

Leaning forward, Gaia hung on to her every word. "What did he do?"

"Claimed it wasn't how it looked. So I asked him if he loved her, and he said he'd made a vow to never love another. He's been waiting for her to come and find him."

Mother Earth winced. "Ouch. I can see why you want to kill him."

"Totally deserved, right?"

"Yes. And no. You have to understand, Xaphan made that vow a long time ago. A very long time. At the time he made it, he was thinking more with his dick than his head. Not his fault. He is a man and we both know where the blood goes when they get horny."

Just the thought of another woman turning him on made her boiling mad. "So what if he made it while sporting a boner? He obviously cared for this woman. He told me he hasn't fucked anyone in three hundred years. Or was that all a lie too?"

"No, he told you the truth. It's been driving Lucifer nuts. Especially since the woman he's been punishing himself over wasn't the paragon of virtue he thought she was."

"She's not in Heaven, is she?"

Taken aback, Gaia's jaw dropped. "What would make you think that?"

"Not me. Him. He says since this Roxanne girl never found him in Hell to free him from his vow and live happily ever after, then she must be in Heaven." Katie rolled her eyes. "As if."

"As if indeed. That slag never came close to a chance for Heaven. He should have known that, especially given she let him up her skirts while unwed. And he wasn't the first."

"So she fooled him. Doesn't change the fact he still loves her." Just saying it aloud caused an ache in her chest.

"Are you sure of that?"

"Of course I am. Why else would he keep a shrine?"

"But he did break his vow when he slept with you."

"He did, didn't he?" Katie brightened for a moment. Then slumped. "But apparently I didn't matter enough because he went home and didn't do a thing about his altar to Roxanne. He's got to die."

"Let's not do something hasty. You still haven't found the dragon, right?"

Katie shook her head. Who could think of completing a quest at a time like this when every atom in her body cried for vengeance?

"Why not wait a little bit? Find the little critter. Return it to the castle before my granddaughter visits and then see how you feel. Maybe Xaphan can explain it. Or make amends. Sometimes, you need to let the ones you care for have a chance to apologize and make up. Trust me, I speak from experience. Luc hasn't always been the best boyfriend."

"But Xaphan hurt me." Her admission emerged plaintive, and she didn't like it one bit.

"I know. Do you think I haven't dealt with heartache

before? I'm involved with the biggest womanizer the universe has known. Just because we're in a happy phase now, doesn't mean we don't have our moments. Lucifer's hurt me. But then again, I've also done my fair share. It doesn't mean we can't be together. And it doesn't mean I have to kill him, even if there's times I want to."

"I'm not you. I don't want to forgive." *I want to kill him. Hurt him like he hurt me.*

"Katie, you can't get rid of everyone who gets close to you. Give Xaphan another chance. What could it hurt?"

"Me." Such a small admission.

"Tell you what. If he truly hurts you, and I mean more than the naughty spanking kind, then I will hold him down myself so you can carve his heart out."

"Promise?"

"Promise."

After a pinkie swear and a hug, Katie left feeling if not better, at least calmer. She didn't have any intention of forgiving Xaphan. However, she did decide she wanted to hear his piss poor excuse before she killed him.

9

SWEEPING the area that formerly contained his shrine, Xaphan brandished his broom like a weapon when the door to his condo smashed open. He relaxed when he recognized his employer stalking in. Then tensed at the glower directed his way. Anytime smoke came from Lucifer's ears, someone got their ass chewed – or roasted. Neither proved pleasant for the recipient.

"What did you do?" his boss asked in a booming voice. Angry, the usually affable Lucifer appeared like a reddish version of the Hulk, in a three-piece Armani suit, because the devil, while crude, always dressed well.

First rule in Hell; never admit to anything. "Do? Could you be more specific?"

"Katie came barging into my office, interrupting my morning sex with Gaia. As if having purple balls isn't bad enough, the two of them ganged up on me and basically kicked me out. Me! From my space. So I'm asking you again, before I tear you apart, limb from limb, what the fuck did you do?"

Rule number two; when caught, pin it on someone else. "Don't blame me. I just took your advice."

"Shit. I was afraid you'd say that." Lucifer shrank in size and flopped on the couch. "Which part?"

It went against the grain to kiss and tell, but when it came to Lucifer, avoiding the issue would result in torture. "I forwent my vow and seduced Katie. Or she seduced me. I'm kind of blurry on the details. I was still a little drunk when it happened the first time."

"First, as in, you went more than one round?"

"Six actually." And yes, he bragged about his prowess with a huge grin.

Lucifer laughed. "Hot damn. I knew you had it in you. She must have really liked your technique, seeing as how she let you live."

"Well, we did have a bit of an iffy moment with a knife this morning, but I talked her down." He still didn't think she would have killed him. Maimed perhaps. Spilt a little blood. But in the end, he was sure she would have held off from a final, devastating stroke.

"If everything is as good as my Gaia's pie, then why was she so mad when she came storming into my office?" Lucifer pinned him in place with his flaming gaze.

Avoiding the penetrating stare, Xaphan fidgeted, wanting to avoid answering. But where could a demon run and hide when the Devil sat on his couch? "Um. Well. Uh. She kind of saw my shrine to Roxanne."

A pair of bushy brows shot up giving Lucifer an almost comical appearance, not that Xaphan laughed. Now didn't seem like the right time. "You still have that thing? Are you fucking stupid? Who lets the woman he's banging see his stalker wall for another?"

"I planned to get rid of it, but she kind of broke in while I was showering. She freaked before I could explain fully, so she might have left with the wrong impression," he admitted, his tone low as the recollection depressed him anew. He'd just found happiness and lost it because of a stupid vow he should never have made. Retrospect – it kicked a demon when he was already down.

"Well, that explains a lot. You messed this one up royally, boy. And why the fuck would you even have a shrine to that bitch, Roxanne, anyway? It's not like she was ever true to you."

Sweeping again, as he needed something to keep his hands busy lest he put holes in his walls, Xaphan stopped and stared at Lucifer. "What are you talking about?"

"Don't tell me you never figured that out? And here I thought you had a glimmer of intelligence. Did it never occur to you the first time Roxanne let you under her skirts to wonder why she wasn't a virgin?"

"She claimed it was from horse riding, it's why she was so frightened about her father's plan to marry her off. She worried a husband would demand an annulment by claiming she was impure."

Lucifer barked. "Ha! I can't believe you swallowed that piss poor excuse. She wasn't a virgin because she spread those thighs for anyone with a sword. That day in the woods, when you saved her from the boar, what do you think she was doing with her guard? Or do all ladies, when attacked by a boar, have only the tops of their dresses ripped, letting their tits hang out?"

Xaphan frowned. "I didn't think of that." It also explained why the guard never drew his sword, and why

EVE LANGLAIS

she didn't have a mark on her. Great. Now he felt even dumber than before.

"You didn't think of a lot of things, with your big head at any rate."

Surely he couldn't have been that wrong? "But she said she loved me. Said we could be together if she didn't have to marry that old man her father brought home from the courts." A pompous old jerk, surrounded by guards, more than Xaphan could possibly defeat on his own, he'd sold his soul to Lucifer for a chance to kill the aging lord and save Roxanne. Free her so they could be together. It didn't work out as planned.

"Fuck, are you gullible. Remind me to tell you about some land I've got for sale later. As for her claim she loved you," Lucifer made a loud buzzing noise. "Wrong. She didn't want to marry the old man, true, but only because she had her eye on another lord. Did you not wonder why she never came to the dungeon? Why no one ever spoke to you and asked you to explain your side of the events before your scheduled execution?"

An execution he'd missed when Lucifer came for him in the dead of night and spirited him away to his new home in Hell. "I never thought of it, actually." He'd assumed her father had her locked down tighter than a nun in a convent. As for not being questioned, wallowing in self-pity, he'd not even thought of it. He knew he was guilty, so it seemed logical everyone else would too.

"Your precious Roxanne is the one who pointed the finger at you. Not only did she tell all that would listen that you killed the lord in cold blood right before her very eyes, but that you'd taken her against her will and ruined her."

Reeling back, Xaphan, despite the heat in the room, felt a bone chilling cold. "She what? No. She wouldn't do that."

"She did. Cried really pretty tears too as she told her father about how you threatened her into silence."

Fuck me! She'd played him like a fiddle. And fucked him over like a whore without any lube. His poor wall suffered the brunt of his anger. Despite the large hole, he didn't feel any better. "Why didn't you tell me this before? Why let me suffer for three hundred years for a vow that meant nothing?"

"Because, I was waiting for you to realize how stupid it was on your own. Of course, I never counted on it taking this long. I even sent the perfect psycho your way in the hopes of waking your stupid ass up. Instead, you messed up. I mean really, who keeps a fucking shrine of an ex-girlfriend in their apartment? I should kill you myself for being so mentally deficient."

"I'll explain it to her."

"Yeah, I don't know if Katie's going to be willing to let you come close enough to do that. She was pretty mad. I think she cares for you, and you let her down. Just like everyone else in her life. Well, except for me. I am perfection incarnate."

"I knew I should have chased her down," he muttered under his breath. But he'd thought it smarter to get rid of the source of her anger before fetching her back and making her listen to how he'd changed. And he had. Changed because of her. Who wanted to keep a vow to a memory when he'd found someone better, someone who didn't make him temper who and what he was? Who intrigued him on more levels than just the sexual ones?

"So what are you going to do?"

Wallow in self-misery? No, he'd already done that for too long. "I'm going to get her back."

"That's my boy. But how? She's not going to stand still and listen to you. Actually, she'll probably try and slit your throat to avoid conversation."

"I'll figure something out. First I need to find her." *Or let her find me.* Given they'd planned to meet up at the portal leading to the mortal world so they could pay a visit to Pete's Emporium, chances were good they'd run into each other. Or, he'd meet the tip of her dagger.

But who cared about a flesh wound when it seemed he'd broken her heart. *I need to fix this. Tell her what she means to me.* Hopefully he could do a convincingly enough job that she wouldn't kill him.

***

PISSED, BUT DETERMINED TO COMPLETE HER TASK FOR Lucifer, the only male she trusted, Katie snuck around the back of the warehouse for Pete's Emporium. Smack dab in the middle of a human city, not the nice part, the store acted as a way station for witches and other beings who wanted to buy specialty items from Hell and the other planes. In reverse, it also acted as an illegal importer of mortal goods to the nine circles.

Just about everyone knew about Pete and his ill-gotten gains, however, even the guards turned a blind eye. Bribes greased many a palm over the years.

What surprised her about Pete's acquisition of the dragon was knowing Lucifer would have to take a personal interest. Had Pete lost his mind? Who stole from the dark lord himself?

Not that she really cared. By crossing that invisible line that everyone knew to avoid, Pete cost himself his life. Killer Katie was in the house, and given her current mood, blood would flow.

Determined to kill him, though, didn't mean she took foolish risks. Big bruisers guarded the entrances, their heavy bodies bulging with fat and muscle. She'd also wagered under their human guises, demons hid, which meant she also had a sorcerer of some type to worry about as only magic users could change a demon's appearance on the mortal plane.

Yay for me. Another being to kill because magic was outlawed on the human side unless Lucifer gave special dispensation. And that happened only with his family and the minions under his direct command.

Palming her knives, Katie watched the two guards having a smoke and exchanging ribald jests. Standing, she threw both of her knives before they even noticed her presence.

Thunk. The daggers sunk into their chests, piercing their hearts. But that wasn't always enough to kill a demon. As brackish blood seeped from the edges of their wounds, she sprinted, pulling another pair of blades from her hip sheaths. Springing up, her magically enhanced knives slid through their flesh, severing tendons and even bone like it was soft butter.

A pair of heads, wearing identical expressions of surprise toppled and hit the ground. Pulling her knives from their bodies, she wiped them clean of the dark coating. She liked to keep her weapons shiny and clean. Yanking some tags from her pockets, she slapped them on the corpses, and their separate heads, sending straight to the swamp where the critters would take care of the bodies.

Habit had her always cleaning up after herself, and Lucifer abetted her fetish to remove the evidence by keeping her well supplied with tags spelled to send whatever she stuck them to into the deepest part of the swamp. When a demon fucked up, in other words pissed the boss – or her – off, there wasn't a funeral or a trial, which totally annoyed the few undertakers trying to make a living in Hell.

Evidence disposed, the back door unguarded, she took a quick peek around, saw nothing suspicious and slipped into the building. She threw her knives before her brain could fully process the situation.

Xaphan ducked and the blades buried themselves to the hilt in the wall.

"What are you doing here?" she snapped.

"Finishing our mission."

"How did you get in? I just took care of the guards outside."

He disappeared and reappeared, close, too close, a half smile curving his lips. "Getting into guarded places is my specialty."

She aimed a kick, but it never connected as he faded from sight and reappeared across the room.

"Still angry, I see."

"Me? Of course not. I don't hold grudges." *I kill them.*

In a move worthy of Matrix, Xaphan contorted his body and the set of flying blades she sent whipping for his heart also missed.

"Well that answers one question. If you'd –" Thunk. "–just let me –" Ping. "–explain." Clang.

"Nothing to explain," she snapped, pulling forth another pair of daggers, small needlelike ones, from the seams of her jeans.

"How many of those do you have?"

"That's for me to know and for your body to find out." She missed again. Dammit!

"You were never meant to see the shrine."

"Obviously. I might be crazy, but I'm not stupid."

"No, you're misunderstanding. I didn't mean to imply I was going to hide it. I was going to get rid of it. You just came over before I had a chance. It's gone now. Incinerated to ashes, something I should have done years ago."

It was? No. She didn't care. Not one bit. "No need to bother on my account. I don't care if you've got a sick obsession with a dead woman. Whatever turns your crank."

"Dammit, stop twisting everything." The door to the employee break room swung open, interrupting their conversation. Before the human, probably another disguised demon, could shout a warning, Xaphan yanked him into the space, kicked the back of the male's knees, sent him to the floor, and decapitated him.

Fuck. Xaphan was so hot when he got violent. Jerk. She didn't want to admire him. He'd hurt her. She wanted to hurt him back. Of course, her body seemed to think riding him like a cowgirl while raking her nails down his chest would suffice.

She scowled. "If you're done yapping, can we finish the job?"

"If by finish, you mean we get the dragon, kill the bad

guys and end up at my place where I get on my knees to show you how sorry I am, either with words or my tongue, then sure."

Okay, she might have swallowed a fly or two, her jaw dropped so low at his brazen statement. "What did you just say?"

He winked. "How about I just show you? Try and keep up. And let's make it interesting. Whoever kills the most villains gets a prize."

"Any prize?" she asked. "Including your head?" She smiled sweetly.

"My *head* is yours anytime you want it, *baby*."

Shocked speechless again, she watched as her formerly grumpy partner, dove through the door.

He challenged me. And propositioned her. She didn't know which threw her off kilter more. But by all the whores in Hell, despite her intrigue at his words, she wasn't about to let him win.

Retrieving her knives first, she pushed through the door and found him standing over a pair of guards, very dead guards.

"Three to two," he cajoled. "You're falling behind already. Do you want me to win that bad?"

"You wish. Stand back and watch how a real killer works a crowd."

"Tease. You know how I enjoy watching you move."

He did? Flustered, she didn't reply, but she couldn't stop the heat from coursing through her limbs.

Avoiding the front of the store where clients – human ones – browsed and the legal part of the business operated, they instead found the locked door leading to the basement.

Pulling a pin from her hair, Katie was about to impress him with her lock picking skills, when he brushed her aside with a rumbled, "Allow me."

Raising a booted foot, he slammed it into the door. With a boom, the portal smashed inward.

"Subtle. Why not ring a bell and let them all know we're coming?"

"I couldn't find one," he admitted. "How's this? Hey assholes, I'm coming to get you!"

Voice booming, he announced their presence, and this time she couldn't help but chuckle. What got into him? Had one night with her completely unbalanced him? While sexy as a grim demon before, the new him as a psycho with killer tendencies really turned her on.

But she still wouldn't let him win.

"Last one down the stairs is a rotten egg," she cried as she jumped onto the rail. With an exuberant, "Whee," down she sailed.

Whipping down the stairs, following a flying blonde ponytail, accompanied by Katie's giggles, Xaphan smiled. *She didn't kill me.* Sure, she'd pretended to try, tossing her little knives at him with seemingly deadly intent. But he'd seen her in action. She could have taken him out if she'd really wanted to. *Yet, she didn't.*

The knowledge elated him. Made him feel light and, oddly, happy. Happy enough, he'd thrown her off kilter by talking dirty for the first time in his life. The expression on her face? So worth it. Even greater, he'd quite enjoyed not holding back.

Freed of his vow, a vow that dragged him down in more ways than he'd realized, he felt like laughing. So he did, a booming guffaw that made the guards he ran into, as he spilled onto the basement level, blanch.

Moving his sword in quick arcs, they didn't even have time to fire their weapons before they decorated the floor.

"That's a total of five for me," he boasted.

Standing over her own set of corpses, Katie stuck her

tongue out at him. "I'm only one behind you, grumpy. And only because you cheated by not letting a lady go first."

"Lady?"

"Yes, lady." She tossed her hair, and dammit, if the teasing grin didn't make him want to shove her up against a wall and kiss her until her eyes crossed.

"You'd carve my balls if I treated you like delicate china. If you ask me, I think you want to lose. I think the idea of getting naked in my bed turns you on. I have a big bed you know. Perfect for what I have planned."

Her breath hitched, her eyes dilated, and she licked her lips before replying. "I'll kill you first."

"Now who's challenging who? You want to kill me so bad, then you better hope you win." He no sooner spoke than thugs poured into the room, some from above whence they'd just arrived, others from the rooms adjoining the one they occupied. Yet more came from the hatch door in the floor, almost in their midst.

Keeping an eye on his psycho – who didn't appear to need help as she danced with her blades, laughing as she killed – Xaphan fought hard to stay ahead of her, each rolling head one point closer to his ultimate goal of getting her back to his place so he could show her she was the one he wanted. Not Roxanne.

The fight went well, despite their smaller numbers – his prowess with a blade and her ability to disarm the enemy with laughter, followed by a knife, meant they were winning. Another three kills each. A sweaty pair. Then as he took care of an annoying, oversized imp who wouldn't stand still, she took out two minor demons who'd shed their human costume. Shit, she caught up.

Tied in numbers, and out of things to kill, they stood in a pool of blood and body parts staring at each other, chests heaving slightly from the exertion, their bodies coated in sweat, among other fluids.

A quick peek around before she faced him again and her lips quirked. "It seems we're at an impasse."

"Why don't you just concede, and make it easier on yourself?"

She laughed. "You're out of your mind."

"Yup. Have been since I met you."

Flustered, she wouldn't meet his gaze. She turned away and moved to crouch by the hatch in the floor. "Wanna bet the bad guy is holed up in his cave?"

"For once, couldn't they have a cottage on the beach? I hate going underground," he grumbled joining her.

"Scared of confined places?" she taunted.

"Nope. I just hate spiders. Damn things have too many legs. It's just not right," he exclaimed.

Admitting that aloud was totally worth it as laughter pealed from her. "That's funny. Remind me to take you to the Dark Woods in the sixth circle sometime. They're not only eight legged, they're hairy."

He didn't have to fake a shudder at her words. "If you're done trying to give me nightmares, let's go finish this. I'm horny, and ready to claim my prize."

"In your dreams demon," she scoffed, but she said it with a sideways glance and a curl to her lips that told him more than words that he affected her. Smirking, she said, "Last one to the bad man's lair is a rotten egg."

Hip checking her aside, Xaphan jumped into the hole first, chuckling at her exclaimed, "Hey! That's cheating!"

"No," he replied, taking a quick peek around before

looking up, "that's called winning." A demon strode from the shadows and lost its head a second later as he swung his word. "That's twelve for me. Start getting naked, baby, because I'm about to exterminate this place."

With those words, he charged into the rock hewn tunnel the now dead demon came from. He couldn't wait to finish. *And claim my prize.*

Nuts. He's completely fucking nuts. And hot. Don't forget hot.

Watching him fight, a mixture of brute strength and skill, proved a panty-wetting experience. He didn't hesitate, he didn't draw it out. He went straight for the kill.

He was so damned good at taking their targets out, she was having a hard time keeping up. More shocking, a part of her wanted him to win. The more he teased her with his dirty intentions, the more she wanted to lay down her knives and declare him the winner.

Madness.

But she still wanted it.

Wanting it though, and letting him win without working for it were two different things. She didn't have it in her to just give up. So, despite him charging ahead, she sprinted after him. Tunneling further than she would have expected underground, with twists and turns, including some side passages, the corridor went on forever and she lost sight of her grumpy demon. Only the fact the jerk left slash marks in the stone, great big 'X's', let her know she followed the right trail.

She heard the sounds of battle and saw the yellow

glow of light long before she spilled into a cavernous room glinting with gold. *Ooh, pretty.* And she didn't mean the piles of gold coins, the tiaras and jewels, either, but the hot demon whose shirt fluttered in tatters giving her glimpses of his awesome chest.

Engaged in battle with a pair of massive trolls, Xaphan held his own, but barely as he danced around the treasure laden room while huge spiked clubs came crashing down on either side of him. Seeing her chance to catch up, Katie threw her daggers in quick succession, great aim putting one through a troll's eye, right into its brain. Boom. Down it went. The heavy thud made the floor vibrate.

The other troll, however, kept bashing, her knife having missed, skipping off its almost armor-like, thick skin.

"About time you joined me," Xaphan said with a nonchalance that belied his dodging of the troll who seemed intent on squishing him like a bug.

"Well, you know me. I had to stop and fix a nail. Battle and monster proof lacquer my sweet ass. So are you going to play with that thing all day, or were you saving it for me?"

Springing up, in a lightning quick move, he swiped his sword, left, then right, before hitting the ground on two feet. "You were saying?" The troll behind him wobbled, then collapsed, his body split into pieces, the giant X on his torso having sliced clean through.

"Nice sword work."

"Wait until you see the stuff I'm going to show you later." He gave her a sexy grin and winked. Dammit it all, a hot heat crept up her cheeks.

Not fair. Throwing her grumpy demon off kilter was supposed to be her thing.

Changing the subject, because the current one left her disarmed, and lacking a response – other than 'Show me now!' – she said, "I see treasure. Towering piles of it. But no dragon. No Pete. And no other doors out of here."

"That won't do. We need another villain to break the tie. Unless you've decided to concede?" He shot her a hopeful look.

She blew him a raspberry in reply.

"So now what?" he asked.

"Maybe the dragon's hiding?"

"Is this what you're looking for?" A dulcet female voice echoed out of nowhere. Tightening her grip on her dagger, Katie scanned the piles of glistening gold, trying to discern the direction of the speaker.

But when the owner of the voice did finally step forth, Katie forgot to throw her knives. Hell, she forgot to breath.

From a behind a stack of chests, holding a heavy, iron link leash connected to one very pink dragon was the woman from Xaphan's shrine. Roxanne. Or as she wanted to call her, the-woman-I'd-like-to-scalp. But maybe she was wrong. Perhaps she just happened to look a lot like her.

Her grumpy demon confirmed her first impression a moment later with a shocked, "Roxanne?"

"Xaphan, my love," exclaimed the dark haired beauty, pressing her hand to her heart. "What a surprise. I never thought I'd see you again."

"I'll bet you didn't," he muttered, not looking at all impressed with her reappearance in his life.

"Don't be angry, my love. I know we promised to find each other in the afterlife, but that was before the horrible deal I made with the devil. How could I return to you when he turned me into a horrible, undead creature?"

Yeah, it must have been horrible to be forever doomed to have pale unblemished skin that accented full, red lips and dark, seductive eyes. Katie clamped her lips tight as the two lovers reunited. It just surprised her that Xaphan didn't drop his sword and immediately run to kiss his beloved. Although, she was glad she didn't. She might have barfed in her mouth before killing them both.

"So, let me see if I understand; you avoided me these last three hundred years because you thought I'd reject you?"

"I should have known better." Roxanne smiled, a radiant expression that made Katie all too aware of how imperfect she was.

Covered in blood, her hair a wild mess and lacking even an ounce of Roxanne's immaculate beauty. And to think, she'd almost allowed herself to believe Xaphan when he so ardently pursued her. *I am such an idiot.* Did her past teach her nothing? Trust no one, especially not males who claimed to care then tried to hurt her.

It stopped now.

Reunited with his lost love, it should have made the decision to win the bet easy. Kill the vampire bitch and then leave Xaphan to his misery. A pain worse than death.

She clutched the hilts of her knives tight. One throw. Just one to make him hurt like she currently did. His gaze brushed hers, an almost pleading look.

Dammit! She couldn't do it. She who'd killed blubbering thieves, whining assassins, and demons with two

144

left feet on the dance floor, couldn't kill one helpless female. *Because if I do, Xaphan will hate me.*

And despite everything, she didn't want him to hate her or to look upon her with revulsion in his eyes. So their contest would end in a tie. As if it mattered anymore. With his precious Roxanne returned, it's not as if he'd want to claim her as a prize, anyway.

The realization was enough to depress even a usually bubbly psycho. To avoid further humiliation, she turned, ready to leave with her cute tush dragging. However, before she could take a step, Xaphan zoomed in on their reason for being there, and she swiveled back to hear the answer.

"What are you doing with the dragon, Roxanne?"

"This creature, she's mine. Someone found her for me in the swamp. Pretty isn't she?"

Katie snorted.

"Very cute, and she's the spitting image of the one that's missing. Or hadn't you heard? Lucifer's been searching for a pink dragon just like this one. His grand-daughter's was stolen."

Katie frowned. Like, hello? The two were obviously one and the same. Why did Xaphan dance around the fact his girlfriend obviously appropriated it? Did his besotted brain lack the ability to see the truth under his nose?

A titter escaped Roxanne. "What a coincidence."

"Is it?"

"Xaphan, my love, surely you don't think me capable of stealing a little girl's pet." It must have taken a lot of practice, but the conniving bitch even managed to summon a few tears. "You know me. I would never do such a thing."

Xaphan's jaw hardened. But he didn't call her out. "Where's Pete?"

A sly expression overtook the fake tearful one. "On vacation. An extended one. He left me in charge while he was gone."

"I see." Again, his words emerged clipped, and as if sensing his distance, Roxanne looped the dragon's leash around a statue and literally glided to him, her hips swaying more than a succubus looking for dinner.

"Darling, I've missed you so much." Roxanne reached up to touch him, and sick to her stomach, Katie turned away. With leaden feet, she walked to the exit.

Stupid rotten, lying, no good...

"Where do you think you're going, my little psycho?" Xaphan demanded in a loud voice. "We're not done yet."

Whirling, Katie fought the tears that threatened to spill. "I'm pretty sure you can take the dragon back on your own. You and Roxanne." She almost gagged on the bitch's name.

"I wasn't talking about our job for Lucifer. There's the matter of a certain wager. We're currently tied."

"So? Don't tell me you're going to let me kill your precious, Roxanne?" Her fingers itched to throw her daggers.

"Xaphan, what is this crazy girl talking about." The vampire slut clutched at him in a way that twisted Katie's heart.

"Shut your piehole, Roxanne. Katie and I are having a conversation. As I was saying, we seem to be tied, my sweet psycho. While a true gentleman would probably leave the choice of who gets the tie breaking kill up to a lady, we both know you're not a lady, and I am no gentleman. Besides, I play to win. Say hello to number thirteen."

Speechless with shock, Katie watched as his sword speared Roxanne, the tip emerging from her back, wet and red.

Holy. Fucking, Hell. He killed her! For me. She almost came in her pants.

11

CLASPING THE BLADE, his ex-lover gasped. "What did you do? Why?"

Looking into Roxanne's perfect features, Xaphan felt nothing. Not a twinge. Nada. Seeing, however, the stricken look on Katie's face when they realized the villain they chased was his ex-girlfriend? Fuck, the shocked and sad expression just about killed him. He knew in that moment he needed to do something big before his psycho ran away again. Something to show Katie that Roxanne no longer meant anything. Death and the chance to win his bet seemed like the perfect solution.

"You seriously have to ask why? Because you're a lying fucking whore. That's why. And besides, I needed to win a bet with a beautiful killer."

Pulling his blade free with a wet sucking sound, he brought his arm back and let it swing. Ending the slag's life, who'd fucked his up in so many ways, felt damned good. Liberating, but not as exciting as what he planned next.

Katie stood still as a statue as he stalked toward her. Without asking permission, he swept her into his arms and plastered a kiss on her lips, a passionate embrace to show her she was the one he wanted. When he let her up to breathe, her eyes glazed and her lips smiling, she said, "Show off."

"I thought you'd appreciate the romantic gesture."

"Most demons would steal a girl pretty rocks."

"I'm not most demons."

"I've noticed. So now what?"

"Now, we go back to Hell. Someone owes me for losing, and I intend to claim my prize."

Her giggle warmed him through and through. "Patience, demon. We need to return someone to their owner first."

With quick strides, he went to the pink dragon and knelt. He unhooked the cruel iron, freeing it, and petted the creature's head. Rumbling, the dragon rubbed against him. "Come," he ordered the little critter. The princess's pet ambled along behind him as he stalked back to Katie, who quirked a smile.

"I think she likes you."

"It's my charm," he said.

"Or the blood," she added pointing to the dragon licking his boot.

Wrinkling his nose, he shook his foot, and a pair of soulful eyes regarded him with reproach. He sighed and let the dragon lick. "If you tell anyone, I'll have to kill you."

"Why tell when I can post it online?"

Glancing away from the tongue cleaning him off, he

was just in time to catch a flash of light as Katie snapped his picture. "You'll pay for that," he growled.

"Promises. Promises. Grab a hold of our blood thirsty friend there would you? It's time to go home."

Linking her arm around his, while he looped an arm around the dragon, she yanked out her handy-dandy amulet, activated it and sent them home.

It seemed to take forever, in his mind at any rate, for them to make their way to the castle. The pink dragon trotted alongside them, happy as could be, snaking out a tongue for the occasional lick. Katie skipped and hummed at his side, acting once again like her usual perky self – with one big difference, her fingers laced through his. As for him, he'd found his grumpy state again. Easy to achieve when he noticed all the male eyes staring over-long at his woman.

And she was his.

Whether she chose to admit it or not – and she would by the time he got done with her – he didn't intend to let her go. Over the course of the past few days, he'd realized a few things. One, hanging out with Katie was never boring. Even when she wore clothes, she stimulated him.

Two, smiling, didn't make his face crack, and Hell didn't freeze over when he laughed. Happiness could belong to him, if he wanted it. And he did.

The third realization? He loved her. Sure, he'd fought it. Tried to stave off the lure of her giggles and chatter. Attempted to ignore how he warmed whenever she drew near. Did his best to pretend it wasn't jealousy assailing him when he wanted to kill everything that so much as looked at her. *I'm in fucking love.* And he couldn't imagine a future, or a life, without her by his side.

The knowledge scared him shitless because while he knew Katie must harbor some affection for him – he did still live after all – he wasn't sure how she'd take the news. Thankfully he could postpone that announcement until after they returned the dragon.

Popping into Lucifer's office, the secretary told them they'd just missed the big man. It seemed his grand-daughter came for a visit and so they'd adjourned to the rock garden.

Impatient now, especially since Katie kept tossing him coy looks over her shoulder, he rushed them to the inner courtyard, and stopped dead in the doorway.

"I'll be damned," he muttered.

"You already are," Katie added. Then she uttered an, "Oooh!" as she saw what caught his attention.

Giggling as she scampered after a bright pink dragon was a little girl with a bow in her hair. Lucifer noticed them and waved them over.

"You're back. Good news. Turns out the dragon wasn't missing after all. Little Lucinda here learned how to make a portal and smuggled Fluffy home. Muriel found it in the shed this morning when she went looking for some pruning shears." Lucifer beamed with pride at his grand-daughter's misdeeds.

Shaking her head, Lucifer's daughter, Muriel, made a face. "The brat. I told her we couldn't keep the dragon on the mortal plane so she thought she'd hide it so she could visit it when she wanted."

"Hold on a second." Xaphan looked down at the pink critter at his side. "If that's the missing pet, then where did this one come from? And what about the tracks we followed into the swamp from the secret tunnel?"

Stopping her play, the little girl fixed him with eyes that sent a shiver down his spine. "I did that," she said in a babyish voice at odds with the knowledge in her gaze. "I couldn't do a portal in the garden, grandpa would have felt it. So I took Fluffy to the bog and then took her home right after I turned one of those smelly frogs into a copy."

"You what?" Muriel yelled, while Lucifer, beaming from ear to ear exclaimed, "That's grandpa's girl!"

As if to prove her seemingly crazy words, Lucinda, who appeared like a four year old but scared the shit out of everyone, stared at the pink dragon licking Xaphan's boot. With a pop, an oversized frog with bulging eyes appeared.

What do you know, as it turned out, Roxanne told the truth, probably for the first time in her undead life. Someone did find a pink – fake – dragon in the swamp and gave it to her. And, with a quick phone call, Lucifer discerned Pete was actually on a well-deserved vacation. Oops. He'd killed Roxanne for crimes she didn't commit. But Xaphan didn't feel any guilt over what he'd done. Given the choice between making Katie realize Roxanne was no longer a factor in his life, or always having her doubt, he would have still chosen the permanent solution.

Mystery solved, and needing to escape as Lucifer entertained his young guest by spinning his head like a top while smoke poured from his nostrils, Xaphan dragged Katie away from the insanity of their overlord and hightailed it to his apartment.

Giggling with laughter, Katie kept pace with him as they raced to the nearest bed. His bed, where he intended to keep her until he mustered the courage to say the phrase, 'I love you.' His biggest worry? The fact she'd probably try to kill him as soon as he dared utter the L word . *I wonder if I should tie her down first.*

Oh, the possibilities, and he didn't just mean the erotic kind.

LIGHTHEARTED, AND HORNY, KATIE DIDN'T PROTEST WHEN Xaphan tossed her onto his large bed. "Whee!"

Already in the process of stripping his shirt, he paused, and stared at her. "What's it going to take to have you make that sound when I'm buried in you?"

A giggle escaped her. "I guess you'll have to experiment and find out."

"Tease."

"Yup." She winked, then grinned wide as he groaned, probably because she grabbed her breasts through her shirt. Her very dirty shirt. She wrinkled her nose. "I need a shower. I'm gross."

"I agree." Grabbing her ankle, he dragged her toward him while she squealed. Scooping her up, he slung her over his shoulder and carted her off to his bathroom. She only got a glimpse of black glass mosaic tile before he turned her upright.

Gently, he set her on his vanity, and proceeded to strip her, tugging her bloody shirt off first, then kneeling to unlace her boots. His slow advance made her heart race and her breath come short. Boots discarded, he peeled her socks while she wiggled impatiently.

"You're taking too long."

Peeking up at her, his jaw already shadowed with a five o'clock bristle, his lips curved into a sensuous grin and her heart stuttered. She could have stared at him all day. But she preferred to fuck him instead.

"I thought patience was a virtue," he calmly stated, standing to unbuckle her pants.

"For those who aren't wet and ready," she retorted.

He stopped the slow shimmy of her jeans over her hips. "Are you –" He swallowed and his voice emerged in a low growl. "– damp for me, Katie?"

A shiver went through her at his question. "Very. I need you, grumpy. So hurry the fuck up?" she finished on a brighter note. But it seemed the hunger consuming her finally got the better of him. With a tearing sound, he tore her pants away leaving her clad only in panties.

A calloused hand cupped her sex and she closed her eyes as the heat of his touch made her tremble. A hard yank was all it took to bare her. She moaned as his finger stroked between her folds.

"You forgot to mention how very hot you are too," he murmured.

"And dirty. So very, very dirty," she purred, leaning forward to run her hands over his bared chest. She hit the waist of his pants and ran a digit along the inside of the band, loving how his stomach muscles tensed. Unbuckling his belt, then slipping his buttons from their loops, she spread his jeans wide and caught him as his cock spilled out, hard and ready.

"Have I mentioned I like you dirty?"

"And I like you inside of me, but we can't always get what we want," she crooned.

"Is that your way of saying we need to shower first because I don't think I can wait that long," he groaned, thrusting his hips and sliding his dick back and forth in her grasp.

Her lips pressed against the smooth skin of his chest and she felt the erratic, fast paced thump of his heart. "Well, you did kind of win the bet, so I guess, I can't really stop you from taking your prize," she whispered against his flesh before nipping it. The cock in her hands swelled. She spread her legs and wrapped them around his waist, tugging him closer, close enough she could rub the tip of him against her sex. He sucked in a breath.

"I thought you weren't going to kill me," he gasped as she dipped him in and out, just enough to wet him.

"I'm not wearing any knives."

"And yet, I think I'm going to die if I don't sink my cock into that sweet pussy of yours," he groaned.

Peeking up, she caught him staring at her, his eyes heavy lidded with passion. "You say the sweetest things," she murmured with a smile.

"Fuck saying. It's time for doing," he retorted before guiding his thick shaft into her sex. Slowly, he sank into her, filling her. He gripped her buttocks and held her in place as he ground himself into her, stroking her sweet spot.

"What about our shower?" she panted.

"You want the shower? I'll give it to you." Keeping her sheathed around his cock, he lifted her from the vanity and stepped into his huge tiled cubicle. Back braced against his wall, she held onto his shoulders and lifted, then dropped herself on him as he fiddled with the knobs. The initial blast of cold water made her yell, and all her muscles clenched.

"Fuck!" Xaphan's hips bucked and her sex tightened

ever further around him. "I'm coming, baby." As if she didn't notice the spurting heat inside her. She'd made him lose control. How awesome was that?

He didn't seem as impressed though. "I'm sorry," he muttered, his head hanging in obvious chagrin. "I needed you too much."

"So we're done?"

"Not on your life," he growled. "This is just the beginning."

NOTHING LIKE COMING BEFORE YOUR WOMAN TO FEEL LIKE a selfish lover, Xaphan thought with disgust. Not that Katie seemed pissed. Actually, she tossed him a sweet smile and a mischievous wink that totally reinforced his revelation that he loved her.

Letting his limp cock slip from her, he set about proving to her in the only way he could think of – that might not get him killed – how much he cared for her. Worshipped her. His own living goddess, er psycho.

Lathering her body with his soap, he started at her shoulders and worked his way down, his hand cupping and kneading her heavy breasts. She just about purred as he strummed her nipples, the taut buds begging for a taste. He dipped for a lick, then spat.

"Damned soap," he cursed.

She giggled. "That's karma teaching you not to talk with a dirty mouth."

Entranced by her laughter, he rinsed the remaining suds and went back to the object of his desire, her sweet red berries.

Her laughter turned into moans of pleasure as he sucked at them, his teeth grazing them as he alternated sucking and licking. But that was just the entrée. Kneeling, he rubbed his face against her soft belly as his hand stroked between her damp folds.

"Xaphan." She whispered his name as he kissed his way lower, nuzzling the top of her mound. He slid a finger in to her sex. Mmm, hot and wet. He slipped another in. Tighter, nice. He pumped his digits in and out, a slow cadence which quickly had her rocking her hips. Then he applied his tongue to her clit.

And nearly lost his hair. She gripped him tight as a cry of pleasure ripped from her. Around his fingers, her whole sex squeezed. Damn but he wanted her to come. Again and again, he flicked his tongue against her nub as he finger fucked her. She bucked. She yelled. She tore at his scalp. She came.

Only someone who'd had a part of themselves inserted in a pussy as it climaxed could understand the magical beauty of it. The uncontrollable shudders of the flesh. The awe that they'd managed to bring a person such body wracking pleasure.

One climax down, hungry for another, he didn't let go. He kept sucking and licking her while his fingers thrust faster into her quivering sex. She tightened again in a way that told him she was building toward her second orgasm.

She must have known it too, because she released her grip on his hair, braced her hands on his shoulders, brought her knee up, and foot flat on his chest, shoved him. He landed on his back on the shower, a little rough, but so worth the landing when she pounced on him.

Perched over him, her hair damp, her eyes shining,

and her lips smiling, she leaned in for a kiss. She devoured his mouth as she lowered herself onto him, her pussy suctioning him in until she sat on him. As she sucked on his tongue, she ground herself against him, pushing him deep, the muscles of channel pulsing, rousing his need for her fast and furious. Lips locked, his hands on her hips, he thrust up, into her as she pushed down onto him.

It was savage. Rough. Beautiful. Perfect. And when she came, crying his name, he couldn't help but follow, the words in his heart slipping free.

"I love you, Katie."

1 2

THE WORDS, 'I LOVE YOU,' echoed all around her. Slapped her. Shocked her. A roaring noise filled her ears. Panic washed over her in a tidal wave of epic proportions.

"No." She squeaked. "No. No. No." She muttered, leaning away from him, their lower bodies still so intimately joined. "Why did you have to say that?" Because he'd done it now. Forced her to recognize how much she loved him, too. Problem was, while she knew what she felt, had no doubts about it – he still lived didn't he? – there was a huge problem with his declaration.

She jumped off him and fled the shower, snagging her ruined clothes on the way.

He of course followed. "Don't freak out. I know you're not into the whole intimacy thing. And you have trust issues."

"I knew I should have killed you," she muttered as she struggled into her dirty shirt. Her pants? Complete and utter write offs. Peering wildly around, she cursed his pristine room. *What kind of man doesn't have clothes lying around?*

"Can't we talk about this?"

"No. I need to go." Quickly before she gave in to the threatening tears.

"Am I pushing you too fast?"

"The speed of light has nothing on you."

"Is it space you need? I'll give you some, but not too much. I'll admit – I'm a jealous guy."

"And I'm a jealous girl," she replied without thinking as she rummaged through his drawers looking for something to cover her bare ass.

"I love you, Katie. I want to be a part of your life."

"You just think you do." Yanking out a pair of track pants, she proceeded to hop into them while doing her best to ignore his dripping, naked body.

"Excuse me?"

"Why? Did you fart?"

"Katie!" he growled. "Don't change the subject by joking. We need to talk about this."

Dressed, of a sorts, in pants wanting to fall and bunch around her ankles, she finally allowed herself to meet his gaze. She almost drowned in it.

Straightening her spine, she took a deep breath. "Fine. You want to talk and know what I think? Here you go. I think you think you're in love with me, but really, you're not. Or won't be. You're on the rebound. You just got out of a three hundred year commitment –"

"I wouldn't call whacking off by myself for a few centuries a commitment," he snapped.

"—and you latched on to the first hot girl you met. Me. Which I can't blame because really, I am adorably cute.

But still. What you're feeling is just lust. Or infatuation. Not love." Okay, so she lost her monotone at the end, the ball of tears in her throat making it hard to speak.

"Bullshit. I know how I feel."

Not caring if he saw her tears anymore, she stalked over to him and poked him in the chest. Ooh, he felt good. She stepped back and shook her finger instead. "You think you know how you feel? Really? Because you thought you loved Roxanne too. Turns out you were wrong about her."

"I was. I'll admit that. But this is different. It feels different. Real. More intense."

"That's just because I'm good. Fuck a few more women, you'll see I'm not that special. Well, actually, I am, but I'm not the woman for you."

"I say you are."

"I drive you nuts."

"But I like it."

"No, you don't. I'm nothing like Roxanne. I'm messy. Disorganized. Sly. Violent. And just plain wrong for you. You need someone with matching eyes that you can put up on a pedestal and worship."

"But I like your eyes, and all those other things. I want to worship you."

Why did he have to sound so sincere? "No you don't!" She stamped her foot. How dare he make this hard? Didn't he see she was trying to do the right thing? Well, the right thing for her at any rate. She couldn't love him. If she did, he'd leave her. Just like her daddy did. Or he'd hurt her like the other men who paraded into her life. She just couldn't allow it.

"You're not making any sense."

"That's because I'm crazy." As she said it, she knocked him out with the butt of a knife that she grabbed from her torn up pants. He slumped to the floor and she immediately felt bad. She fetched him a pillow. Then a blanket, more to cover up his yummy manparts than keep him warm.

Staring down at his unconscious face, so handsome, even with the bruise blossoming on his temple, she sighed.

Dammit. Why did he have to ruin great sex by pretending he possessed feelings for her? He couldn't have just given her a few orgasms and walked away, allowing her to hate him and thus get over him by killing him. Oh no. He wanted her to think he could love her. That they could have a happily ever after. As if.

Katie knew better. Or so she told herself. Deep down, she understood it was fear that made her react so violently. A fear of trust. A fear she just couldn't help, or handle.

Dressed, if oddly, she left, after doing one more thing to him, without glancing back. She fled his apartment and his life. Escaped everything that reminded her of him. The one thing she couldn't shake? Her love for him and the depression that followed. But she and melancholy were old friends, so at least she wasn't alone.

Xaphan woke to a headache and limbs stretched in discomfort. What the fuck? Craning his head, he noted the blanket tucked around him, the pillow under his head, and the ribbons of his sheets knotted around his extremities, holding him in place.

Did Katie seriously think such paltry methods could hold him captive? He barely flexed and he snapped the makeshift bonds. Popping to his feet, he knew without even looking, she'd left. He scared her with his declaration, just as he feared. But, it didn't sadden him because he discovered something really important.

Katie cared for him. Dare he even hope, she loved him? What else to think given his head remained attached, his body parts were intact, and the fact she'd cared enough to cover him before she fled?

Problem was, he realized a few hours later, where had she fled *to*?

All his searching resulted in failure. Depressed, he sank onto the stone steps in the main hall of Lucifer's castle and moped.

"Why the sad face?"

At Mother Earth's query, Xaphan jumped to his feet and snapped to attention.

"Just pensive, ma'am."

"Where's Katie?"

"Gone," he admitted, unable to hide his glum tone.

"She couldn't handle your love, could she?"

He stared at her in astonishment. How did she know?

Gaia rolled her eyes. "Oh don't look at me like that. It's obvious the two of you were falling for each other. I was hoping, though, that Katie wouldn't panic."

"Why did she? I mean, I told her I loved her."

"You have to understand, Xaphan, Katie wants to trust you. But, in her life, men have always let her down. Her own daddy, who claimed to love her more than anything, walked out on her. Her step daddies treated her horribly, as did pretty much all the men she ever encountered. Even her own mother let her down."

"But I wouldn't. I'm a man of my word. Or was," he amended.

A sly smile graced Gaia's lips. "Yes, I heard you broke your vow. But I'd say keeping it for three hundred years without cheating still makes you a man of honor. It's the thing Lucifer hates most about you."

"How do I find her and get her to believe me?"

"Do you truly love her?"

"Yes." No hesitation. Just knowing she was out there, hurting, and alone, drove him crazy.

"Then, follow your heart."

Follow his heart? But the last time it led him astray.

"Woman!" Lucifer bellowed striding into the hall wearing polished, black Hessians. "Stop meddling with my minion. Xaphan, ignore her. And buck up, man. The game is not lost. Ricco has a hound ready when you are to pick up her trail. First though, you need to come with me."

"Why, sir?"

"So I can prepare you for the fight of your life," Lucifer exclaimed.

His brow creased. "You think I'll have to battle her?"

Xaphan didn't duck and thus got the full impact of the smack Lucifer gave him on the back of his head. "Idiot. I'm not talking about a fight with your fists. This is a woman's heart we're talking about. You need to go in and win a battle of the mind and heart. Good thing for you, I have the tactics and intel you need to succeed."

"Or he could just follow his heart," Gaia yelled after them.

Xaphan and Lucifer shared a look – then snorted. Xaphan was sticking with the Devil who knew women and had a concrete plan. *Because I am not letting you go, Katie. Ready or not, I'm coming for you.*

13

ONE DAY PASSED. Two. Then three. He didn't show up.

It shouldn't have surprised Katie. After all, she'd technically dumped him, thrown his declaration of love in his face. Knocked him unconscious. Oh, and tied him to his furniture. Hell, for all she knew, he was still bound there, pride keeping him from calling for aid.

But still, if he truly loved her as he claimed, nothing would have kept him away. So what if she'd travelled to the darkest corner of the Dark Woods and hidden her trail? Sure, she'd gone to the one place sure to give him the willies, an arachnid infested territory with webs large enough to swallow a demon alive, cocooning him for a future meal. Intentional? Well duh. It seemed only fitting in her panic that she squirrel herself away in the place where his greatest fears dwelled. Giant, eight legged, hairy monsters.

Despite her claim that he couldn't love her, that he just rebounded, a part of her, despite herself, believed he'd come and find her. That he'd arrive, stern faced and angry, ready to shake some sense into her. Then fuck her until she promised to never leave again.

Foolish dream. She'd thought herself too mature for that type of fantasy. And yet, no matter how often she chided herself for being a fool, she still perked up whenever she heard a branch crack or the webs rustled.

Three days though. More than enough time to locate her if he truly wanted to. He obviously didn't.

Sitting on her branch, swinging a leg, she sighed. *And to think, I almost believed him when he said he loved me.*

Arms wrapped around her upper body, rigid bands of steel, trapping her arms.

"What the fuck!" she yelled. She'd not heard even a whisper of sound or movement before getting trapped by – she looked down, and her heart pounded – a grumpy, yet sexy, demon. *He came for me!*

"Hello," Xaphan purred in her ear, a husky murmur that shot tingles to her toes.

"How did you sneak up on me?" she asked, not ready to face him, not with her whole body – heart and mind – bursting with joy at his arrival.

"Master of shadows, remember?"

"But, I hid my tracks."

"I borrowed a friend's nose."

"I'm in the center of spider territory."

"Yeah. I noticed. Good thing I brought a big can of arachnid spray."

She bit back a giggle at the thought of him fighting off spiders with a giant red can of Raid. "It took you three days to follow," she accused.

"I was busy."

Busy doing what? Chasing other girls? Trying to forget her? "Well, you're too late."

"Too late for what?"

"To have me. I'm not interested."

"Yes, you are. I missed you. Did you miss me?" he murmured, his breath tickling her ear.

He missed her? Her heart pattered faster. "Nope. I didn't miss you at all. Not even a teeny tiny bit."

"Liar." He chuckled as he turned her in his grasp until she faced him, still trapped in the cage of his arms.

"Why did you come?"

"Because I love you." He slapped a hand over her mouth before she could retort. "No. You don't get to talk yet. You have a tendency, I noticed, of flying off the handle with wrong conclusions, so this time you need to listen. I love you, Katie, killer of demons and sexy psycho."

She shook her head behind his enforced silence.

"Don't try and deny it. I know what I'm feeling. And I'm telling you right now I never felt it before."

She narrowed her gaze.

"Never. What I had with Roxanne was nothing like what I feel for you. Not even close. I need you."

No, she wouldn't melt. She had to stay strong.

"Stubborn, psycho. Fine, you need more proof? I went to the bars the first day after you left."

Aha, the cheater.

"I let women hit on me, left, right and center."

Oh, she could feel a murderous rampage coming on.

"They left me cold."

Killing spree averted.

"So I went to a dating service."

Blood pressure rising.

"They introduced me to beautiful women, nice women."

Going to explode.

"None of them could hold a candle to you."

Out went her breath.

"I know I'm trust worthy, and you should too. I spent three hundred years not noticing a damned woman, and believe me, many tried to get in my pants. None, not a single fucking one though ever gave me sleepless nights. None, not even Roxanne, ever had me rubbing my dick until it was raw. None made me want to smile again. Until you."

She could feel the shield around her resolve slipping. She crazy glued it back in place with thoughts of murder and mayhem. Hell was about to have a female shortage.

"A while ago, you told me if I truly loved Roxanne, I would have known the little things about her. Well, I didn't love her. But I can prove I love you." Sitting down on the ground, he didn't give her a choice but to sit in his lap. Sure, she could have fought, drawn a knife and relieved him of some blood, but...she wanted to hear what he had to say.

"Your favorite color isn't pink like you wear all the time, but purple. All your underwear is purple, as are your sheets, and towels. Even your damned dishes are some girly mauve color. But I guess I better get used to eating on them since I don't intend to leave you."

Okay, so he'd snooped and guessed. It meant nothing. Anyone looking could have figured that out.

"Just so you know," he continued. "You will be moving in with me since my place is bigger. I've already called a painter in to paint the bedroom purple, but if you tell anyone, I'll divulge the fact you secretly watch American Idol."

Her eyes widened. He wouldn't? Hmm, judging by the twitch in his lips, yeah, he would. Damn, but she liked his style.

"Your favorite food, which I will state right now is one of mine too, is crispy fried chicken with mashed potatoes, gravy, and biscuits. Although, I might recommend we mix it up sometime with some baguette, French of course."

Again, too easy. Her last meal before her execution was a matter of record, a record he took the time to look up before coming. It meant nothing. Even she didn't believe that.

"You love the Venus flytrap because it reminds you of your favorite movie, Little Shop Of Horrors. You want to name your first child Jennifer, just because you like it."

She did.

"Your favorite dessert is coconut cream pie with extra whipped cream. You like your coffee with three sugars and lots of cream. You take your bagel toasted with double cream cheese. You hate girl movies. Love to sing Madonna when you're alone. Oh and you think that werewolf dude from True Blood is hot. Which by the way won't be true for long because I'm going to kick his ass so fucking hard, he'll never leave his house again and he'll get fat and ugly." He released her mouth.

"No need to get all medieval on Alcide's butt. Your ass is much cuter."

"That's all you have to say?"

She shrugged. Okay, so he'd figured out a whole bunch of her secrets. He'd made an effort. It didn't mean...oh fuck it. Who was she kidding? She loved the demon and if he didn't love her then he was faking it real good. And if he ever hurt her? She'd carve his ass into so many pieces a baby demon wouldn't choke when fed them. "You forgot one thing."

"No, I didn't." He cupped her face and caught her gaze. "You have a dream, a dream of falling in love with someone who will never hurt you. Never betray you. Who would rather die than leave you. You want someone you can trust and love. That person is me. I'm your dream, and you're my reason for living."

"Fine. I admit it. I love you. But just so you know, just because I love you doesn't mean I won't carve your heart out if you ever look at a woman with lusty intent."

"My sweet, violent psycho, I feel the same way."

Nothing screamed made-for-each-other-couple like matching murderous tendencies.

"So what now?"

"Now, we go home, together. Because this is forever, baby."

"'Til death do us part?"

"Fuck that. I'll follow you in whatever afterlife there is for demons and psychos."

She laughed. "Okay. Seal it with a kiss?"

"In just a second. Since you love me, I have a task for you."

"What?" she asked leaning in close, waiting for her kiss.

"Can you get us out of here? I ran out of bug spray and I'm pretty sure I made the inhabitants of this creepy place mad." Xaphan regarded the shadows, laced in cobwebs, with suspicion.

Laughing, and keeping his attention averted, lest he

see the enormous hairy arachnid hovering, over his head, she embraced him as she activated her amulet.

While their lovemaking ended up delayed due to their matching jealous rage when a succubus dared wink at him, and a demon turned around to check out her ass, while they made their way to his apartment, it was everything she could hope for. Naked, hot, sweaty, full of love and a little blood.

As for the impromptu tattoo she gave him – 'Property of Katie' carved into his chest – he wore it with pride, once he stopped yelling that was.

And though she still had anger issues, an anger shifted mostly to females who dared flirt with him, she was no longer alone. Loved by her grumpy demon – with anger issues of his own mixed with a healthy dose of jealousy – she finally found her Prince Charming, and her happily ever after.

EPILOGUE

"HE FOUND HER, and guess what? She didn't kill him." Lucifer rubbed his hands in glee as his newest matchmaking endeavor passed with flying colors.

"I'm glad for Katie although I still can't believe you got Xaphan to forgo his vow, even before he knew about Roxanne's slutty ways."

"I know. I am the king of awesome. Do I get a prize?"

"You just got a prize."

So he had, Lucifer thought with a fond smile as he stroked Gaia's naked hip. "I think I need another one."

"In a bit, you randy devil. So tell me, who's next on your matchmaking agenda?"

Not getting some, even if he stood at attention tenting the sheet, he laced his hands under his head. "How do you know I'm not done?"

A laugh trilled forth. "Oh please. You haven't had this much fun since the Crusades."

"And just how would you know? We weren't even dating at the time."

An enigmatic smile graced her lips. "Ah, but I had my eye on you. Even though we were in an off period, I always kept tabs on you. Don't tell me you thought all those sandstorms messing with your infidels were flukes?"

"Stalker."

"I prefer the label well informed. So, who's next?"

"I was thinking of killing two numskulls with one golf ball. Felipe and Zancia. What do you think about me making them both my new caddies for the upcoming gold match?"

"Ysabel's pet cat and a water demon." She said it musingly. "Aren't you afraid of pissing your witch off?"

"Nah. She's too busy driving Remy mental to notice anything else at the moment. And besides, someone needs to rein that feline in."

"Felipe challenged you didn't he?"

"The damned beast had the nerve to steal the cheese soufflé chef made for me!" And he'd so looked forward to his treat.

"So you're going to reward him by fixing him up with a girl?"

"Depends on your definition of reward. He's determined to stay a single tomcat. But I want some shifters in my army. And as one of the few left of her kind, Zancia needs to come out of her shell."

"Are you sure about those two? You know cats hate water. And Zancia has got to be the most timid thing I've ever seen."

"Exactly. It's perfect." What could be better than a shapeshifter and a siren?"

"But still, using them as your caddies? I thought you wanted to win?"

"I do. Fuck. Maybe I should hold off on that pair." His cock wilted at the thought of losing. Gaia was right. He needed a caddy. A good one. And quick, the tournament wasn't far away. The solution came to him in a blinding flash of insight. "I know who to use."

"Tell me."

"McGregor. That ornery bastard has been hiding somewhere along the river. I'll force him out of retirement to caddy for me, whether he likes it or not. I know just the gal to do it. And to *do* him." He whispered the name in her ear.

"Oh you're just evil," Gaia giggled.

"I know. It's a gift," he boasted before tackling Gaia to the mattress for round two.

Later on, he couldn't help smiling at his choices for the next contestants in Hell's mating game. Sure, they'd probably kick and scream at first, but in the end, the lucky couples would thank him – and if they didn't he'd post a video of their courtship on Helltube.

Plans to rebuild his army were moving along nicely. And even luckier for him, Lucifer would snag McGregor, the greatest golfer Hell ever saw – after him, of course – to caddy.

His generosity truly was stunning. So what if McGregor swore he'd never play again? He'd do as his Lord commanded, or else! With Luck locked in the west tower, and Karma in the eastern one, nothing could stop him from winning. The cup for the winner of the Golf Across The Planes tournament was going to look great on his mantle – and would make an awesome mug for drinking grog.

The End (of this story)
But the fun continues...Date With Death

Made in the USA
Coppell, TX
24 March 2020

17606993R00098